I AM NOT OK

K. LUCAS

I AM NOT NOAH

A NOVEL

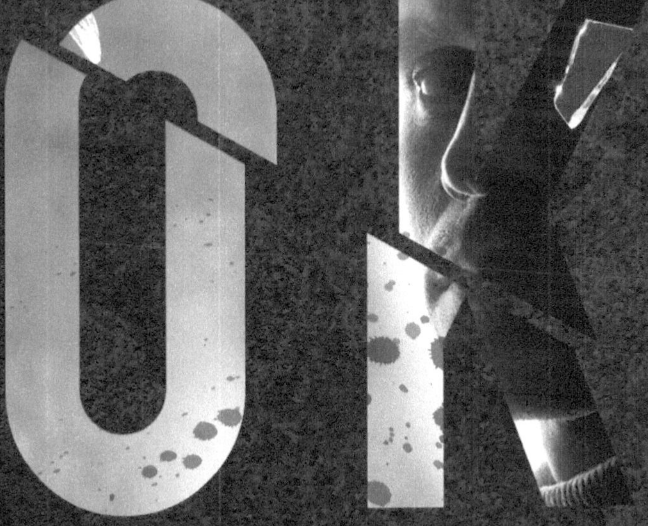

K. LUCAS

EBook ISBN: 978-1-958445-00-6

Paperback ISBN: 979-8-9850093-3-0

Hardback ISBN: 978-1-958445-90-7

Cover Design by Pretty In Ink Creations

Editing and Proofreading by My Brother's Editor

For my son

ED

NOW

am OK, I think, taking a deep breath. I exhale slowly, adding to the thought—*everything is going to be alright*. I think it again, willing myself to believe it, continuing the thought over and over in my mind. If I think it enough times, I'll feel it eventually.

I lay on the top bunk, numb. The ceiling stares back at me, also numb. A dirty white that makes me feel old and used up. I bring my hands in front of my face. The blood has stained my skin. I'm not sure whose it is. No matter how many times I've scrubbed—it's still there. I wonder if it will be on me forever.

The hours blend in a haze. I don't know how long it's been since they died. I'm not sure I really care but it's all that seems to be on my mind. Them dying. Images of blood-soaked carpet flash before my eyes. I clench them shut, trying to block the memories out. There are so many blank spots. Why do I have to remember *this*?

I tell myself there's only one thing I care about now—making sure Em is okay. This is all my fault and I'm locked up away from her. She *needs* me. How is she going to manage with me in here? Is *Doug* going to take care of her? I could almost laugh at the thought. Almost.

I've been waiting for her to come see me. She hasn't. After what happened, I don't blame her, but I need her to. I wish we were the kind of twins like in the movies, where they share a sort of psychic telepathy. What I would give to be able to summon her to me with my thoughts.

A guard passes my cell with loud footsteps, making his rounds. He stops to stare at me. "In the mood to talk today?" he asks.

I say nothing.

He waits for me to speak. Then he moves on. I won't say anything to *them*. Not until I speak with Em first.

When the court-appointed attorney meets with me, my silence infuriates him. "You need to speak to me, Mr. Daniels," he says, trying to contain his anger. His eyes flash when I don't answer. It's funny, but I don't have the urge to smile. I want to ask him about my sister, but I can't. Not yet.

"If you don't tell me your side, I can't defend you," he continues.

I stare at a spot that stands out on the faded white walls. It's brown. I wonder if it's a spot of old, dried-up coffee, or maybe someone's blood. I think about other brown things —food, *feces*...

"Are you listening to me?" my attorney demands.

I swivel my head back to meet his gaze.

"Don't you want to defend yourself?"

When I turn my neck again, back to the brown spot on the wall, he sighs in resignation. "Probably for the best anyway. I don't think there's any getting you out of this mess unless we go with an insanity plea."

Insanity. The word rings through my mind like an unwelcome bell, making me flinch. I *hate* that word. It frightens me.

They take me back to my cell, where I'm thankful to be alone. It's all I've ever wanted really, and I'm glad to not be with a group of others.

This is where you're going to be for the rest of your life, Ed. Get used to it.

I picture myself in ten years, then twenty, reading a book by the barred window. I won't have to speak to a soul if I don't feel like it. If others want to cause trouble, I'll let them kill me. It might not come to that if they let me stay alone. I wonder if people can volunteer for solitary confinement or if I have to do something to make them put me there.

Images of the knife come unbidden, dripping blood. Piercing screams fill my mind. I hold my hands over my ears, clench my eyes shut. I pound my hands against the sides of my head, trying to get my brain to process a different thought. *Any* other thought.

I am OK, I remind myself. *Everything is going to be alright —as long as Em is okay.*

ED

THEN

am OK, I think, inhaling as deep as my lungs will allow. *Everything is going to be alright,* I add to the thought, exhaling slow and steady.

"One more time," my therapist says.

In… *I am OK,* out… *Everything is going to be alright.*

"Good. Now, how do you feel?"

As I look into her robotic gaze, I wonder, *Do you even remember my name without looking at my chart?* "Better," I say, giving her a small smile.

"Breathing exercises can be a great tool to help get emotions under control. Have you ever looked into or tried yoga?"

My face scrunches at the thought. I'm unable to envision myself doing *yoga,* although I realize how popular the exercise is. "I prefer to walk," I say.

She nods. "Walking is good, too. It's important to get at least thirty minutes of daily exercise. It will help tremendously."

I give an inward sigh, checking her recommendations off in my head. *Breathing, exercise—check, check. Is any of this really going to help?* "Okay, got it."

Her eyes dart to the clock hanging above my head. She's calculating the minutes we have left—how much longer she has to sit here and listen to my boring life, my boring *problems*. I take a slow, deep breath inward, listening to the tick... tick... tick... as the seconds pass.

"Do you want to tell me about your job?" she asks. "Where do you work?"

There must be more time left in our session.

"I work for All-Star Electric."

Her eyes light up. "Oh, an electrician?"

"No. Call center."

And her eyes dim again. "That must be stressful."

Hence, why I'm here. "Yes. It can be."

"Are you married?"

"No."

"Significant other?"

"No."

"How does it make you feel to be single?"

I swallow the lump in my throat as I think about how to answer. *What kind of question is that anyway?* "I'm not sure," I start. "I mean, I don't particularly want to be single. It's not like I'm against marriage. It just hasn't happened."

She turns back to glance at her computer monitor. "You're twenty- four. Is that right... Edward?"

Ed. "Yes."

Her eyes flick to the clock again. "Well, it looks like our time is up for today. Practice those exercises we talked about, and I want you to think about some things that make you happy. We'll talk about it next time."

As she rises from her chair, I stand to shake her hand. "Thank you," I say, trying to be polite, even though this has been a total waste of my time. I wonder how many repeat clients this woman actually gets.

When I start my car, the clock on the dash reads 5:59 p.m. I try to smile, but it feels more like a grimace. *She couldn't stand to listen to me for another minute.* My chest feels heavy. I try to take a deep breath the way she instructed but it doesn't seem to hold a candle to the feeling burning inside.

I shift the car into reverse. I rack my brain, trying to decide where to go next. There *is* no place *to* go. I don't want to go home, and I don't start work again until tomorrow morning. I'm sure my sister would love for me to visit, but that's not going to happen, either.

The car seems to drive itself as I find myself traveling through streets only vaguely familiar. I flip the visor down, blocking the sun from burning my eyes. The next thing I know, I'm sitting on a bench overlooking the Puget Sound.

Red and orange rays light up the water and the horizon. The sunset is beautiful today. I breathe slowly and deeply in… *I am OK,* and out… *everything is going to be alright.* I try it a second time but am unable to finish the final thought before I feel nauseous. I lean forward on the bench, putting my head between my knees, before trying again. In… *I am OK,* out… Everything—

"Hey, are you okay?" a stranger's voice calls. I look up with wide eyes, my face heating from embarrassment. I glance around for a moment, not seeing anyone. Then I realize there's a woman at the other end of the field, by the playground. She's looking at a child who fell. *Not talking to me.*

It doesn't matter. I'm done making myself look like a fool, even if I'm invisible to everyone around. I get up from the bench, ready to head back to the car, but I stop short. *Why not go for that walk?*

The walking path is staring at me, daring me. I don't feel like it; I don't want to. It's going to be dark soon. I think about going home, then I start for the trail.

EMMIE

THEN

My phone is ringing *again.* She won't stop calling. I sigh before answering. "Hi, Mom."

"Emersyn, have you heard from your brother?" Her voice is like nails on a chalkboard—grating my spine the whole way down.

"No, not today. Why?"

"He's not home yet. I thought he might be with you."

"Why do you always think I know where he is?"

Her laugh is condescending. "You're his twin, silly. You usually *do* know where he is."

Just because I'm his twin, it does not make me his keeper. "Have you tried calling him?"

"No," she sighs. "You know he never answers his phone."

Only for you, Mom. "I'm sure he's fine. He's probably out with friends from work or something."

She laughs again. "You know Edward doesn't have any friends."

"That's not—"

"Anyway, let me know if he shows up, will you? I'm worried."

"Mom—"

"Love you, honey. Bye!"

She ends the call before I can get a word in to defend him. She's always doing this—trying to check in on him like he's a child. My brother is a twenty-four-year-old grown man, and our mother treats him like a ten-year-old.

I know it's driving him insane. I can see it in his eyes when he's around her. I need to try harder next time. I need to say *something* to make her understand what she's doing to him.

I make my way back to the kitchen to finish making dinner. While I'm eating, I check my messages to confirm Eddie hasn't tried contacting me. There's nothing. Sometimes I wonder if he loves me as much as I love him.

Maybe I'm bugging him as much as our mom is. I think about sending him a text to check in, but I don't want to be as bad as her. I open my messenger app to start typing. **Hey Eddie, thinking of you! How's your week going?**

The words stare back at me as I read them, reread, and then reread again. I delete them and type again. **Hey Ed, how's it going?** I know he hates when I call him "Eddie." But that's what I always call him and maybe I'll come off the wrong way if I *don't* call him that, even though I know he hates it.

I delete the message again, to start over. *Should I just not text him at all?* I toss my phone onto the couch and walk away, message left unsent. I'll call Eddie tomorrow. It will be better that way, and I'll be able to tell by the tone of his voice if he's lying to me.

As I lie awake, trying desperately to fall asleep, I toss and turn with excitement and nerves. There's a secret I'm keeping from my family—one that will change all our lives.

I'm worried about how to tell them. Daddy can be really old-school and I'm not in the mood for a lecture from him. Mom will be thrilled, I'm sure. But Eddie—I'm worried about him the most.

I don't want my happiness to bring him lower and I'm afraid that's exactly what's going to happen. I don't want this to come between us, so I have to tread lightly. It's what keeps me up at night and has for the past week. *How am I going to tell him?*

My phone buzzes on the nightstand after I've just flopped onto my other side for the twentieth time. Sighing, I turn over to reach for it.

Hey beautiful, the message says.

I don't even try to fight the grin that appears on my face.

Hey, you, I text back.

Three dots appear, and then a new message. **Up late? Sorry to wake you.**

No, I just can't sleep, I reply. **Too excited!**

My phone starts ringing. I answer, "Hey, I thought you were working."

"I am, but I just wanted to hear your voice and tell you good night."

I'm glad he can't see me grinning from ear to ear like a schoolgirl, cheeks bright red, I'm sure. "Good night," I say.

"How are you feeling?"

"I was a little sick today, but fine now."

"I wish there was something I could do to help," he says.

"You can hurry up with your shift and come home to me."

"Girl, you know I'm counting down the minutes until I clock out."

I laugh. "I know."

"Uh-huh, you better. Good night for real. I'll see you soon."

Butterflies in my stomach now, I don't know how I'm ever going to get to sleep. There's something about that man that I just can't get enough of. My smile falters when I think, *I hope Eddie loves him as much as I do.*

I feel like a failure. *I wasn't able to help him. I didn't do enough. I could have tried harder.* It didn't have to come to this. The thoughts make me want to scream, want to pull my hair out. I throw my books off the bookshelf, my lamp across the floor. I swing the cupboard doors open in the kitchen, and toss out dish after dish, relishing the earsplitting sound of the breaking ceramics.

"You could cut yourself on those," Doug says.

I look over at him, wondering if he's warning me or *telling* me.

"This is your fault," I whisper.

"Don't blame me."

"I do blame you!" I cry. I want to throw something at his head, but I know I'll miss. "You left me!"

He doesn't respond, doesn't move.

"Leave me alone!" I scream.

He stares at me with a blank expression. He won't go anywhere. Not until he's ready.

"What do I have to do to get you out of my life?" I plead with him, hating myself at the same time for speaking the words. There's a part of me deep inside that can't believe I even had such a thought, let alone spoke it out loud.

"Stop wasting your breath. And you're going to hurt my child. You need to be more careful."

My hand moves to my stomach. I'm still not showing, but it shouldn't be long now before I do. A protective instinct claws its way forward. *I can't do anything to hurt the baby.*

I hate that Doug is right. I need to calm down, even if I don't want to. I take deep, steady breaths, trying to calm my racing heart. Tears won't stop falling, no matter how hard I try. I blow my nose, wipe my face, and more come.

"Eddie!" I scream, falling to the floor on top of the broken dishes. "Eddie!"

"You need to cut that shit out," Doug says, moving toward me. I think he's going to offer me a hand up, but he doesn't. He looms over me, staring uselessly. I wish he would go. *I wish he would hold me.*

Seeing my brother taken in handcuffs broke a piece of my soul. I'm not sure how I'm supposed to ever get over this. *All the blood.* All I ever wanted was for him to be okay. Now, he's as far from it as possible.

"I need to see him." I stand up and move toward the bedroom to get cleaned up. It's not too late for me to be there for him.

"I don't think so," Doug says.

"I don't care what you say, Doug. I'm seeing my brother."

"It's too soon."

I turn on him. He was following me into the bedroom, and I push him away from me. "Stop!"

"Listen to me, Emmie." He grabs hold of my shoulders and shakes me. "You know I'm right."

I shake my head, refusing to listen. "No. You're not.

He's scared, he's hurting. After—what happened." I choke back bile. "He needs me now more than ever."

"He needs to get acquainted with his new situation."

"His new—Doug! I need to help him defend himself. He needs help. We need to make sure they don't throw him in with the wolves."

"You may not be able to see him right away anyway. It takes hours, sometimes days, to process people. Maybe even longer. At best, you'll just be sitting there, waiting. At worst, they'll send you home."

"I have to try. I'm not going to abandon him."

"You're not—"

"I am! If I stay here and do nothing, I am."

Doug looks at me with that blank stare that I hate. His eyes look like pools of black, drawing me into them. I could stare at them for hours even though the emptiness is frightening.

I shake my head at the thought. *Emptiness?* Doug's eyes never look empty. I look at him again. They're blue, not black. He's smiling, understanding. It's like looking at a completely different person than I was moments ago.

"I'll go with you," he says.

"Th-thank you."

"We need to eat first, though. If we're going to be waiting there for hours, then I'd rather not be starving."

I can't even think about food at a time like this. My stomach is in knots. I don't know how he can worry about something so trivial, but I don't argue. I've done enough of that.

"I'll fix us something while you get ready," he says.

I nod and watch him leave the bedroom. I've never been afraid of Doug before. I'm not sure if that's the name for this feeling starting to overwhelm me, but whatever it is, I try to push it back down to wherever it came from.

ED
THEN

I find myself at the grocery store—one last ditch effort to kill time before going home. In the cereal aisle, there's a woman who seems to be looking at me. I try not to look back at her, but out of the corner of my eye, I can't help but feel her eyes on me.

Maybe I'm wrong, maybe she's just looking in my direction, not *at* me. I glance over my shoulder. She's standing behind an empty shopping cart, staring right at me. She's not even pretending to hide it. *What's her problem?* I don't know if I should say something or if she's just a wacko that I should ignore.

She doesn't look like a wacko. She looks gorgeous, with long straight brown hair that I want to run my fingers through. I can't see her eyes from here, but they look dark. She looks flawless and silent. There's nothing awkward about her demeanor. She's just calm and still and *looking at me.*

I test her by walking to one side of the aisle, then switching to the other. Her eyes follow me. It's uncomfortable to have someone looking at me like this; I'm unused to the attention. My palms grow damp, but I'm not sure why. All she's doing is looking.

I'm trying to work up the nerve to say something; why would a woman, *anyone* for that matter, be staring at *me*? Maybe I have something on me. I run a hand over the top of my head and then across my face.

I grab a random box of cereal, then turn back toward the stranger, ready to finally confront her. She's gone. No trace of her left. I go to the end of the aisle, peek out both directions, but she seems to have vanished.

Grocery shopping is a huge waste of time. You'll never change my mind on that. We spend time strolling up and down the aisles, looking for food to fill up our shopping carts, only to go home and put everything away, before eating it all in an hour.

I suppose I'm lucky enough to not really need to do it. Stopping here every night means I only buy enough for a day at a time. And the only food I really need is for lunch, anyway. It's mainly just a little time killer built into my schedule—one of many.

I push the shopping cart toward the bakery. The smell of freshly baked bread always wafts in the air there, filling me with temporary comfort. I meander along through the store, grabbing this and that—things I don't really need.

A man and woman with their arms around each other, step to the end of an aisle. They look both ways before stepping out in front of me, almost walking straight into my side. It's not the first time it's happened and won't be the last.

I head toward the produce, thinking about the woman who was staring at me, as I examine a red apple. Then, I feel a jolt of pain in my heel and jerk forward as a cart rams into me from behind.

"Oh god, I'm sorry!" a lady cries out, rushing toward me, eyes full of worry.

I'm more full of shock than pain. Her cart hadn't knocked me down or anything, just tripped me and pinned me between it and the apples. "It's okay, no worries," I say. I try to smile but it comes out in an awkward grimace.

Her eyes grow wide in surprise and suddenly I feel like a moron because I realize the woman hadn't even noticed my presence. She was worried about her toddler, who was sitting in the cart. Not me. She glances at me, gives a tentative smile in return to mine then, without a word, pushes her cart away.

Blushing, I sigh, then head for the registers. At the checkout, the cashier asks, "Did you have a great shopping experience with us?" His voice drones like a robot. There would've been more enthusiasm from the virtual assistant built into my phone. He's had to have asked this question a million times by now and it's obvious he doesn't enjoy his job.

Right there with you, buddy.

For a brief moment, I consider telling him "No." What if I told him the truth—that I had a terrible experience today? I wonder what he would say. Has anyone ever bothered to give him the truth? I doubt it. It's more of a rhetorical question anyway, just like when someone asks, "How are you?" No one ever wants to hear, "I'm shitty, and you?" It's just not how society works.

I answer him, "Yes, thanks," then enter my shopper club number.

He glances at the screen. "Thank you for shopping with us, Mr. Daniels."

After putting my bags in my cart, I make my way toward the parking lot as fast as I can without running. My hands clench around the handle of the cart, knuckles turning white. I'm so angry with myself for not speaking up. *Why is it so hard?*

The memory of everything that just happened inside

plays over in my mind, and I know that my brain will obsess over it for the rest of the night and probably the rest of the week. There's no doubt I'll lose sleep, thinking about what I should've done or should've said but didn't have the courage to. Even worse than that, are the unwanted thoughts that will come—of what *they* must think of me.

The couple that didn't see me. The woman who wouldn't stop staring at the freak who couldn't decide which cereal to get. The mother whose cart got away from her, who had some creep try to talk to her. The cashier who was too disinterested to pay attention to the nobody who was paying for his groceries. Would any of them give me a second thought? Probably not. I wish I could say the same about them.

Six o'clock in the morning takes an eternity to arrive for an insomniac. My brain has this problem where it won't shut up and let me sleep, so I'm tortured all night by my thoughts while I wait for my alarm to release me from my self-induced prison.

With purple rings under my eyes, I get ready for the day, determined to do something different. *Today is the day*, I remind myself, just like I do every other day. I weigh the idea of calling in sick. I've never done it before; I'm not even sure what I would say. *Would they believe me? Would they even care?* I shake my head at the thought. What else would I do with my time?

As I pour myself a cup of coffee, I remember my therapist appointment. *That was something different.* And the walk at sunset. *That was different too.* I feel a small smile form on my lips and I'm shocked because I can't remember the last time I smiled at myself, proud of an achievement.

"What are you smiling at?"

I look up from my coffee to see *him* walking into the kitchen. He pads across the floor in his boxers and bare chest, rubbing the sleep from his eyes.

"Nothing," I say, moving away from the coffee pot.

"Did you finally get laid last night?"

My cheeks turn scarlet. I move to leave the kitchen, foregoing making my lunch for the day. He doesn't expect me to answer, anyway.

"Your mother was worried sick," he says.

"Sorry," I mumble, almost to the front door now.

"Don't walk away from me when I'm talking to you, goddammit!"

I stop in my tracks with one hand on the doorknob. Sometimes I think he sets his alarm just so he can catch me before I leave for work. This is his *fun* that he looks forward to all day long, until the next morning.

Turning back around to face him, I brace myself for what comes next. "Sorry," I say again.

"Come over here and talk to me a minute."

"I really have to get going—"

"I said come sit the fuck down."

I try to hide my trembling hands in my pockets as I walk back into the kitchen to sit at the table. I can't look at his face; I know what I'll see there, and it will break me before I even start the day.

"I'll call Mom to apologize later," I offer.

"Uh-huh. You do that."

He stands there in front of the coffee pot, drinking from his cup, looking out the window. The seconds tick by. I ask myself for the millionth time, *Why the hell am I still here? Why am I putting up with this shit day after day?* There is no answer. I have no answer for myself.

"Dad, I really should get going. Can we chat tonight?" I ask, keeping my eyes trained anywhere but his face.

He comes to the table, sitting in the chair next to me. "You want to *chat*?" he sneers. "You think that's what this is?"

"I—Well, I—"

"I-I-I-I, fuck boy, when are you going to move the hell out of here? Look at you! Pathetic."

"I—"

He slaps me upside the head, making me fall backward in my chair. "Again, with the fucking 'I!'" He sets his steaming cup on the table in front of me, and before I can think, he pushes it over, spilling the scorching liquid over my arms, chest, and lap.

Searing pain shoots through me. I yank back and stand up as fast as I can, sucking in breaths, trying to stay calm. I know better than to cry out.

"Oops, sorry, champ," he says.

I meet his gaze, unable to resist anymore. His eyes are gleaming like the cat that got the cream, daring me to say something. I stare at him, wishing I had the nerve to confront him, wishing my life wasn't like this. *Why does he hate me so much? Why don't I just leave?*

If I confront him in a calm, rational manner, and say, "You know that was no accident," he'd probably throw the whole pot in my face and laugh. "Nope! Sure wasn't!" I'm not in the mood to confront him. I *never* am, and he knows it. *What is wrong with me?*

Tears are pooling in my eyes, but I can't let him see. It would give him too much satisfaction and give him one more reason to look down on me. I run back to my room to change into fresh clothes, and rather than have to face him again, I crawl through my bedroom window to head to work.

The things I do to make my mother happy, I think as I pull up to the curb in front of their house. Every week I take a day to go visit *like a good daughter*. If I admit the truth, I *like* to visit with them. Most of the time, anyway. It's nice to have a close relationship with my parents.

And if I'm *really* telling the truth, maybe I'm just as bad as my mom. Because what I really want, is to get the updates on Eddie. My mom usually knows *everything*, and if I didn't come over to chat, I would know almost nothing about what's happening in my brother's life.

As I climb out of the car and slam the door shut behind me, I look up to see someone climbing out of one of my parents' windows. Panic rises in my chest. *Holy shit, are they being robbed?* I'm about to scream when I notice it's not just someone—it's Eddie.

"Eddie?" I call from across the lawn.

He turns toward me and when I see the panic in his eyes, my heart jumps to my throat. When he puts a finger over his mouth, motioning for me to be quiet, I race to him, worried that something is terribly wrong.

"What's going on?" I whisper.

"Shh. Follow me."

He leads me to the far corner of the front yard, where we can't be seen from the front window, and from there we go back down to the street. "We have to be quiet," he says.

"Eddie, what's going on? You're scaring me."

He sighs. "Nothing is going on. It's fine. I just didn't want *him* to hear us."

"Him? You mean Daddy?"

"Like I said. *Him.*"

My eyebrows furrow. I know Eddie and our dad don't have a good relationship. Everyone knows it. Daddy can be a dick to Eddie and doesn't even try to hide it. "What did he do now?"

Eddie shakes his head. "Doesn't matter. Good to see you, Em." He gives me a tight hug, then says, "I have to go to work. I'm late."

"But it's Saturday."

"Overtime."

"Eddie—"

He flinches at my use of the nickname that he hates.

"Sorry. *Ed*, don't you ever get a day off?"

He laughs, walking away now. "A day off to do what? Get killed by *him*? No thanks. I'd rather spend my time making money."

"What are you talking about? Eddie—*Ed,* what did he do to you?"

"Nothing!" he calls, almost to his car now. "I'll talk to you later."

"You could get a hobby! You don't have to be home, but you don't have to work yourself to death either!"

He waves, acknowledging he heard me, as he climbs into the driver's seat and starts the car. As I watch my brother drive away, I can't help but think about the situation.

Eddie was seriously *climbing out of a window*. He's afraid of our dad. *Is he really that afraid of him?* What is Daddy doing to him to make it get to this point? And he made that other comment, too. Does he really think our dad is going to try killing him? Of course Daddy would never do something like that—but if Eddie is so afraid that he thinks he *could*—that's worse than I ever imagined.

I clench my fists at my sides, hating to see my brother living like this. *No one* should have to live like this, especially not Eddie. He's such a good person—so gentle and kind to everyone. I wonder if Mom knows what's going on between them.

Determined to confront both my parents, I make my way to their front door.

"Hey baby girl!" my dad greets me before I even ring the doorbell and I wonder if he was able to see us the whole time.

"Hi Daddy," I say with a false smile before hugging him.

He steps to the side, ushering me in. "Your mom is just waking up. She should be out in a few minutes. Can I get you a cup of coffee?"

"That would be great." As I follow him into the kitchen, I see paper towels all over the floor by the table. "What happened here?" I ask.

"Oh, just a little spill."

He's smiling at me, offering me a warm mug with an outstretched hand. I can't help but analyze his face. *There's something he's hiding.* His smile looks fake. His eyes are dull. *What is he doing to Eddie?*

"Thanks." I take a sip of the warm coffee. It's just right, like always. We both turn our heads as Mom walks in.

"Emersyn! I didn't know you were here, darling. I'm sorry I wasn't up sooner."

"Hi Mom. I've only been here a minute." Hugging her

feels like home. As I breathe in her familiar, calming scent, I wonder how much she's actually aware of.

"Well, Larry, at least one of our grown children still loves us." She kisses me on the cheek before going to pour herself a cup of coffee.

Daddy laughs but what she said isn't funny. "Mom, don't say things like that."

"Oh, you know I'm just kidding."

"I know, but it's not right. You know Eddie is having a hard time right now."

She winces. "Don't call him that."

"Why are you defending him?" Daddy interjects. "He's a big boy. If he feels he's mistreated, he can stand up for himself."

"He's not here to defend himself right now."

Mom laughs. "Larry, you know how the twins are," she says, referring to the connection that my brother and I share.

"Uh-huh. I'm going to take a shower." He gives me a kiss on the cheek before leaving the room.

When he's gone, I take the chance to interrogate my mom. "Mom, is there something going on that I don't know about?"

Her eyebrows raise over her mug. "Like what?"

"Like between Daddy and Ed—Edward."

She frowns. "Not that I'm aware of. Is there something *you* know that *I* don't?"

"I think Daddy might be bullying him."

She waves her hand in the air. "You know they've been going at it for years."

"I think it's more than that though. And why do you let him treat Eddie that way?"

"I don't *let* your father do anything. You should know that by now."

"Maybe you can't stop him, but you could do something."

"And what would you like me to do, Emersyn?" my mom asks, now raising her voice. I can tell she's getting annoyed with this conversation, but I won't let up. She *should* be annoyed. She should be annoyed every time her husband *bullies* her only son.

"Have you ever said anything to him? Ever asked him to show a little restraint?"

"Of course I have."

I glare at her, not believing a word she's saying. There's not a time I can remember where she ever tried standing up to my father, although she could have him wrapped around her pinky finger if she tried.

"Why are you bringing all this up today anyway? I thought you came to have a nice visit."

"I saw him climbing out the window when I pulled up."

"Who? Your father?"

I sigh. "Eddie, Mom."

"I told you I don't like that name." She gives me a look. "Why was Edward climbing out a window?"

"I think he's afraid of Daddy. Or Daddy did something to him. I don't know."

She laughs. "I can imagine how silly he must've looked."

I glare at her, trying to rein myself in. "Mom, this is serious."

"Oh, stop. If your brother was that terrorized, he would move out. He obviously doesn't care." She holds my hands, brushing her thumbs across the backs of them in a soothing circular motion. "Your brother isn't as sensitive as you are, dear."

I pull my hands away. "Why do you think that? Because he's a man? And men aren't allowed to have emotions?"

She frowns at me. "Of course not."

"I don't know how you can be so blind." I stand up and walk toward the front door.

"Emersyn—"

"I'm sorry, Mom. I don't want to argue. Tell Daddy bye for me."

It's the first time I can remember walking out on her. I've never done anything like this before, but it feels good to stand up for Eddie. I can hear Doug's voice telling me, "I'm so proud of you for standing up to her."

Even from the time we first started seeing each other, he's urged me to assert myself more, especially to my mom. I'm glad to be taking his advice. It feels good. Maybe she will understand how serious this is and take it more seriously. She has to understand that she's the only one who can do anything about the way Daddy treats him.

ED
THEN

Em is standing there, in my rearview mirror, looking like she wants to cry. My eyes shift back to the road. *She's the only person in the entire world who cares.* Sometimes I think that it's only because we shared our mom's uterus at the same time. If we would've been born at different times—maybe she would hate me like everyone else. If things were different, maybe *I* would be the perfect one, and everyone would hate *her*.

On the way to work, in between avoiding accidents and being cut off, I can't help asking myself over and over, "Why don't you just move out?" There are lots of reasons, and yet there's really none. I can say that I stay at home because the price of rent is too high, or that I'm saving up to buy a house, or that I'm there to help my parents as they're aging, or even that I'm currently looking for a place and just haven't found anything yet.

All of those would be lies. I make good money, especially with all the overtime I put in. I have enough to rent a place. I also have some money saved and could buy a house if I chose to. It would actually be pretty easy for me to do.

And I'm sure as hell not still at home to help my parents. I want nothing to do with either of them, and they feel the same about me. It's more like *he* is making it his life's mission to terrorize me and finds some kind of sick pleasure out of it. So, *why* won't I move out? The answer: I just can't.

I walk into my building, heading toward the elevator. A couple of coworkers are standing inside, having a conversation as the elevator doors start to close. I hurry, trying to make it before the doors shut. "Hold the doors!" I call, but I'm too late.

Neither of them made a move to hold the doors open for me. Neither has even glanced in my direction as they slide shut. I move toward the stairs. My cubicle is on the fourth floor. It's not that bad, and I could use the exercise.

As I come out of the stairwell out of breath, my coworkers step out of the elevator. They walk in front of me —neither blinking an eye in my direction. I continue toward my desk with a fake smile plastered to my face.

"Good morning," I say, passing a group of people chatting.

No one says a word as I pass.

At my desk, I sit and get ready to clock in for the day. Some of the others in my unit already have their headsets on and are taking calls. Before I log in, the smell of Brooke's perfume wafts toward me as she walks by. I close my eyes and breathe it in.

"Good morning, Ed," she says as she passes. She's in the next cubicle over, and most days, she is what gets me through my shift. She's also one of the only other people who actually call me what I want to be called. Not *Eddie*, or *Edward*. Ed. Plain old Ed—just like I like.

"Morning Brooke," I respond as she sits down.

"In for a little overtime, too, I see."

"Yeah. Never pass on the chance for more money," I say with a smile, wanting to kick myself at how stupid I sound to my own ears.

She gives a weak smile and turns to her computer.

Brooke is another part of my life that I do nothing about. She's the kindest, sweetest person and actually *sees* me, but she's also kind to *everyone*. I'm not stupid. I know that there's nothing special between us, and I'd be a fool to ask her out. Why would a woman like her want to be with a man like me? Someone who still lives with his parents. Forget the parents. Why would a woman like her want to be with someone who's *invisible*? Knowing it's impossible doesn't stop me from dreaming, though.

I put my headset on and take the first call. "Thank you for calling All-Star Electric. How can I help you today?"

"How can you help me? You can make my fucking electric bill go away. That's what you can goddamn do!"

I put the call on mute before letting out a deep sigh. I can tell today is going to be *such* a great day. *Just like every other day.*

When calls are slow, I glance across the divider to watch Brooke. She's talking to some lucky caller on the other end of her line, a smile on her face, chatting like they're best friends. *How can she love her job so much?*

I wonder if any callers ever speak to Brooke the way they do to me. The thought makes me angry. I *hope* they don't. Brooke doesn't deserve that kind of treatment. I can't imagine someone yelling at her through her headset, *cussing* at her, *threatening* her, calling her all kinds of foul names. A part of me feels like all the belligerent callers are routed to me, which would explain why she's always smiling.

Brooke laughs and brushes her hair back before typing something on the screen and making a few clicks of the mouse. Her eyes scan back and forth, reading something. *Can she see me watching from the corner of her eye?* I look away before we make eye contact.

My headset dings as another call comes through. I go through the motions on autopilot, taking call after call, the same thing over and over. All the while, half of my brain is in another reality.

I imagine myself taking Brooke out for lunch. We take an hour-long break, instead of the usual thirty minutes. As we sit at some restaurant—maybe one overlooking the water—I say something funny to make her smile that *smile* —the one that drives me wild. Her eyes are shining as she looks at me, and I can tell she wants to go out again.

We stand together outside our office building, ready to go back inside and finish the rest of the day. She leans in to kiss me. I wrap my arms around her back, pulling her closer, managing not to screw it up.

I see us starting a life together. I buy us a house—any one she wants. I get her a dog. I get her anything she dreams of—*anything* to make her happy. A sense of peace fills me. We're in love. Nothing else matters.

I'm jolted back to reality when the alarm on my computer goes off, telling me to clock out for lunch. I take my headset off and spend a minute deciding if I'll eat lunch in the car today or sit in the break room. Then I remember what happened this morning. I wasn't able to pack a lunch. Looks like I'm headed to the cafeteria to buy something.

I'm the first one in the elevator. I punch the number 2 button and watch the doors start to close. "Hold it!" someone calls.

I stick my hand out to stop the doors, catching a glimpse of a person reaching out. Out of breath, Brooke steps in. "Thanks, Ed." She smiles at me, and I think I might pass out.

"No problem," I say, then pull out my phone and

pretend to do something important. The seconds tick by as a cold sweat breaks out on my forehead. *This is so awkward.* I want to say something to her, but I'm clueless. I rack my brain, silently praying for some epiphany that will allow me to speak with this woman.

Her scent fills up the small space. Is it jasmine? A bead of sweat is dripping down my forehead but I'm too nervous to wipe it away. From the corner of my eye, I see her looking at me. *Does she want me to say something?* The doors open and we step out.

The feeling of breathlessness takes over, making me feel like I'm suffocating. I can tell that Brooke is heading for the cafeteria too. I'm trying to get enough oxygen in me to think, but I'm starting to see black spots. Instead of following her, I turn to go to the men's room. Entering the single stall, I sit on the toilet and try not to hyperventilate. *What she must think of me.*

I can avoid any more awkwardness by just going to my car. I can probably find a bag of chips shoved under a seat or I can drive down to a fast-food joint. I won't have to see her again, won't have to sit there and look at her from the corner of my eye, won't have to hear Eric flirting with her, won't have to think of anything to say. There's a huge part of me that wants nothing more than the escape. But when I think about it, I get angry.

Is this really my life? I'm too nervous—so I run away? I know it's who I am, but it's not who I *want* to be. It's so hard to fight my own nature, but I have to start somewhere, don't I? This isn't the first time I've had this conversation with myself. Closing my eyes, I bring back the daydream of my life with Brooke. I picture the look on her face just before we kiss. *That's* what I want out of life.

Taking a deep breath, I leave the bathroom and walk toward the cafeteria.

EMMIE

THEN

After leaving my parents' house, I drive around aimlessly, trying to cool my temper. I'm normally not hot headed, but sometimes my mom knows exactly what to say to change that. I take slow, deep breaths, trying to focus on the here and now, but I can't get Eddie's words out of my mind.

A day off to do what? Get killed by him?

And then my dad's tone when he asked, *Why are you defending him?*

I can't shake the feeling Mom is being a little too casual about this. They all are. Why is everyone taking this so lightly? Eddie should not have to be afraid of *anyone*, especially not our dad!

I hit my breaks hard as the light switches from yellow to red. The car behind me honks. *Pay attention to the road, Emmie!*

Today has gone all wrong. Visiting with my parents was supposed to be a good thing. I was supposed to tell them about Doug and me—share happy news, not get into an argument about Eddie.

My fingers grip the steering wheel as I try to release some of the tension. Things are so much worse than I imagined. I've been too self-absorbed, too worried about my own life, and not enough about my brother. *I should be protecting him.*

I vow to myself that I'm going to start trying harder now. I'm going to keep an eye out for him more. I'm going to do what I should've been doing all along.

Back at home, I'm alone again. Just like Eddie, Doug is always working. It's hard sometimes being in a relationship with someone who works nights and trying to adjust to their schedule. When he does overtime on the weekends, it's dayshift. I'm not sure how he gets any sleep, or how he's able to do it, but he seems to be holding up fine.

"I'm doing it for us," he always says when I ask, referring to the extra income that the overtime brings.

"You don't have to worry about that," I always say back. "I have a job too; I can take care of myself."

"I *want* to take care of you. Besides, I'm planning for our future," he never fails to counter, ending any further discussion about it.

Doug doesn't seem to realize that to me, an extra day of his attention would be worth more money than he could ever bring home. We've been seeing each other for a long time, but somehow it feels shorter—almost new. *Probably because of all the time we spend apart.*

He's surprised me before—shown up when he said he was going to be working. It made my day when he did that. Part of me was hoping I would see him in bed sleeping when I got home today.

Just as I'm thinking about him, my phone vibrates. I smile at the caller ID before answering. "Hey you."

"Hey yourself, beautiful. I miss that gorgeous smile."

I'm blushing, still not used to all the compliments he lavishes on me. "I miss you too. How's work?"

"Oh, you know, another day in paradise." He laughs before asking, "So how's the parents?"

"Didn't go so well. I basically argued with my mom the whole time. You'd be proud of me though—I stood up to her for a change."

There's silence on the line. I look at my phone to make sure the call didn't get dropped. He's still there.

"Doug?"

"You know—you don't have to go over there every week. Maybe it will be good for you to get some space from them," he says. "You need to think about your health, Emmie." The cheerful tone is gone; he's serious now.

I sigh, disappointed that I ruined his good mood. Anytime he thinks I'm being mistreated, it doesn't matter by whom or if it's not even true, he gets upset. He's protective of me. It's nice, but I don't like him suggesting I spend less time with my parents. They're my family.

"It wasn't really a big deal, just a misunderstanding about Eddie," I say, trying to lighten the mood. "Anyway, can I make you dinner tonight?"

"How about you let me treat you instead?"

"That sounds great. What time will you be off?"

Before he can respond, there's a beep on my phone that makes me look at the screen. My mom is calling. I hit ignore just as Doug says, "I'll be there around six."

"Can't wait."

When I end the call, I see my cat coming toward me from down the hallway. "Meow," he says, yawning. He leans his front paws forward and does a full body stretch, before continuing to me and rubbing his face against my shins.

"Hi, Shadow," I say, smiling.

He purrs against me and then looks up at me with his glowing yellow eyes, before walking away to his food bowl.

"Love you too, handsome."

I look back down at my phone, still in my hand. *Why would my mom call me?* There's no voice mail. She *never* apologizes, definitely not the reason. After this morning, I'm not really in the mood to call her back.

The person I *should* call, is Eddie. I need to get to the bottom of what's happening with him. He needs to accept that I'm not our mom and that I'm not trying to control him. I only want to be there to help.

Eddie is my favorite person in the entire world. He means so much to me, and I hate when he pushes me away. Yes, I'm his *sister*, but so what. Who cares? Brothers and sisters can still be close, can't they? It's not like we're kids and he's going to get teased for talking to me.

I know he's at work, but maybe I'll catch him on break —or maybe he'll at least listen to a voice mail. Determined to reach him one way or another, I unlock my screen and dial his number.

ED
THEN

Just as I imagined, Eric is there, sitting next to her. My fists clench on their own. He's sitting so close to her it looks like their noses might touch. He's smiling at Brooke like a cat that's about to pounce on its prey. I flush at the sight, hating him, hating *myself.*

Is it me or does it seem she's putting him off? Eric's hand comes up to rest on Brooke's shoulder. It looks like she's trying to lean away from him. She's not smiling like he is, that's for sure. Her laugh sounds forced. *He's making her uncomfortable.* Brooke's eyes scan the room, as if she's looking for an escape.

I can go sit by her. But I haven't got any food yet and might look like an even bigger fool if I sit down empty-handed. I'm kind of starving too. *But what about her?* If she's really in an awkward situation, just my presence might help her. *But what if I'm wrong?* Maybe he's just telling her an unpleasant story.

Maybe it's all in my imagination. I can walk away now, go get in line to get some food. My stomach growls at the thought, liking the idea. I look at the line and then back to Brooke. *What's the worst that can happen?*

Letting out a deep breath, I walk up to Brooke and Eric, and sit down at their table. "Hey guys," I say with false confidence. Both look at me with startled eyes, like I was the last thing in the world either expected to see. Simultaneously, I want to laugh out loud and curl up into a ball. When neither of them says a word, I try again, "How's the salad, Brooke?"

"The—" She looks down. "Oh. It's great."

Now she's smiling. *Is that relief in her eyes?*

Eric chimes in, "You can grab some over there, champ."

Did he just call me champ?

He tilts his head toward the salad bar, in a not so subtle "get lost" gesture. Brooke's smile disappears. Her eyes dart between the two of us.

"No thanks, not hungry today," I lie, trying to keep from grinding my teeth, but I don't think he can miss the irritation in my voice.

Eric's eyes flash. He wasn't expecting defiance. Normally, I would give up at this point and walk away, but today something's different. Maybe it's from seeing the therapist. I didn't think she helped, but maybe I was wrong. Maybe I need to see her again if I'm this different after only one session.

Brooke looks like she's about to say something, but Eric isn't paying attention. He speaks before she has the chance. "If you're not going to eat, what are you doing here?"

I look down at the lunch box in front of him that's not opened. "Well…" *Think, think, think.* "I didn't really feel like taking my lunch break in my cubicle." *Why am I explaining myself to him, like a child?*

"You could take a walk outside." He says it in such an innocent way, like he's trying to offer an old friend a helpful suggestion. My face burns. Too embarrassed to look at Brooke, I look away. When I do, I spot a few people from Eric's unit, at a table together.

"You know," I say, turning back toward Eric, "I almost forgot. I promised Adam that if I saw you, I would let you know, he wanted to see you as soon as possible."

Eric perks up like a dog that's just seen a bone. It was no secret he put in for a promotion, and Adam is the hiring manager. "What? How long ago?"

"Just before I headed downstairs."

"Thanks, champ." *That name again!* Eric leaves without another word to either of us.

Brooke's eyes twinkle. She is probably aware of how full of shit I am at the moment. She knows that when I clocked out for lunch, I went straight for the elevator—do not pass go, do not collect two hundred dollars. *There was no message from Adam.*

"Thanks. I thought he'd never leave," she says.

I can't believe I was right. He really was bothering her, and I'd had the courage to do something about it. There's a feeling inside me that's unfamiliar, swelling in my chest. I almost can't identify it. Is it *pride*? Whatever it is, it's *amazing* and I could really get used to it.

Brooke is looking at me, waiting. I try to fight the grin from showing on my face, but it's hard to do. Part of me wants to scream from elation at winning a battle against Eric, and the other part from the terror of now being all alone with her and having nothing intelligent to say.

As I think about how to respond to Brooke, she gets up and walks away without another word. I took too long. A needle has been taken to my overfilled balloon and I deflate instantly.

"Time to clock in!" she calls back to me.

Is it really time to go back? It seems like I just clocked out minutes ago. *Maybe she just wants to get away from me.* That's probably it. My stomach rumbles as I glance at the clock. Five minutes left. Not enough time to eat. I feel shrunken and hallow, and worst of all, like a fool. *Did I really think she'd want to talk to me?*

I sigh before getting up and picking a bag of chips out of the vending machine. Looks like this will have to do for now.

As I'm getting ready to walk toward the elevator, my phone vibrates in my pocket. I look down at the screen to see my sister calling.

He declined my call. *Again.* I clench my fist around my phone, blood on the verge of boiling. I can feel the anger radiating off me. Shadow looks at me with those eyes again. *He must sense it too.*

I get up to make myself busy, leaving my phone on the couch. Ten minutes later, I try to call Eddie again. This time straight to voice mail without ringing. *He shut his phone off.*

I take a deep breath and then another. "It's okay," I tell myself. "He's just working." *But what if he's not?* What if he just told me that, to give himself somewhere to be? What if he's really *not* at work and instead, he's doing something to hurt himself—because he's too afraid of going home?

Dread rises in my chest as I think about what Eddie might be doing. "I'm not Mom," I remind myself. "I'm not his keeper. It's none of my business what he's doing." But it's not about what he's doing. It's about the fact that I'll never forget finding him with a bloody razor in the bathroom.

This wouldn't be the first time he's hurt himself. *If that's even what he's doing!* I can't take this anymore. I have to find out if my brother is ok. *This is too much like before, for me to live with myself.*

I dial the number for his work.

"Thank you for calling All-Star Electric. How can I help you today?" a voice answers. It's feminine and definitely *not* Eddie.

"Hi, I need to be transferred to Edward Daniels, please."

"Sure, one moment."

Music plays as I'm put on hold. I feel like I'm holding my breath, waiting for someone to say something. If Eddie isn't there, I'm not sure how I'm going to find him.

Finally, the music stops playing. "Thank you for calling All-Star Electric. How can I help you today?"

"Eddie?"

There's a pause. "Em?"

"Eddie, oh my god, you're okay." I exhale, tears threatening to fall. I was worked up for nothing and I'm not sure I've ever been so relieved to hear my brother's voice.

"What's going on?" he asks. "Of course I'm okay. Are *you* okay, Em?"

"I'm sorry. Everything's fine. When I couldn't get a hold of you, I had it in my head that something happened."

"I'm fine." He's short with me; I can tell he's annoyed that I'm calling him at work. "Em, these calls are monitored, you know that. You can't call me at work, unless it's for a legitimate business reason."

My cheeks heat at his tone. He doesn't understand how worried I was, regardless of if it was completely unfounded. Can't he empathize with me a little? "I'm sorry, Eddie. I'll go. But I do need to speak with you. Will you call me tonight, please?"

"Yeah," he says. Then, "Thank you for calling. Have a nice day."

The call ends and the tears I was holding back fall.

I smile across the table at Doug, trying to ignore the stares that we're getting. It seems like anywhere we go together, we never fail to get constant unwanted attention. He's gorgeous, so I can't blame everyone else for wanting to look, but at the same time it's a little nerve-racking—and awkward to be the object of everyone's attention.

"They're staring at us," I whisper through gritted teeth.

He chuckles. "I'm surprised you're not used to it, being so pleasing to the eye." He wiggles his eyebrows at me, and I flush bright red.

"I'm pretty sure it's *you* they're staring at, not me."

"No way."

I smile and reach across to hold his hands. "Let's agree to disagree."

The waiter comes over to our table. "Can I get you something to drink?" he asks. He's blushing, fidgeting, and looking severely uncomfortable.

Doug arches his brow at me, and I shrug. "I'll take a beer," Doug says.

"I'll just have water," I add.

When we're alone again, I glance around the restaurant. *This is so awkward.* "Doug, this is worse than normal."

He smiles and leans back in his chair. "I don't mind it. Do you?"

I give a tight smile back. I don't want to ruin our evening together. "Kind of, yeah. But it's okay. Let's talk about something else."

"Do you want to get our food to go? We can eat at home?"

"No." I shake my head. "I'm tired of just eating at home. This is nice."

"Okay, if you're sure."

"I am. Now, tell me all about your day. I need to get my mind off Eddie."

"What's wrong with Eddie?"

I laugh. "I said I need to get my mind *off* of him, not on him. I don't feel like talking about it tonight."

He smiles again before indulging me in a story about some guys at work doing stupid stuff throughout the day. In the middle of his story, my phone vibrates. I look down to see that it's Eddie. *He's calling me, just like he promised.*

I look back up to Doug. "I have to take this. It's Eddie."

He nods.

I get up and walk to the restroom, where it's quieter, answering as I walk. "Eddie?"

"Do you want to meet? We can talk for a while—if you want, that is."

My heart breaks at how unsure he sounds. "I would love that, Eddie. I'm just at dinner now, can we meet in a couple of hours?"

I hear his hesitation, so I add, "Or you can come over, if you want. You can go to my place and wait there, if you need a place to go."

"Okay. Okay, yeah, I'll go to your place and wait for you."

"Perfect, I'll be there as soon as I'm through with dinner."

I make my way back to the table, but when I get there, it's being cleared. I furrow my brow, confused and angry that they would just assume we were done without even ordering.

Doug isn't at the table. I look around for him, but he's nowhere to be seen. I'm starting to feel like an idiot standing here alone, watching my table be cleared, so I head for the hostess at the front.

"I'm sorry, the server thought you were done," she says.

"I just got up to go to the bathroom. My boyfriend was still at the table."

She looks worried, flips through some papers on her podium. "I'm sorry," she says again. "The server didn't say. He just said he thought you decided not to order."

I glare at her, unable to believe this is actually happening. I'm more mad that Doug isn't up here waiting for me, though. Where could he be? I don't want to yell at this girl; it's not her fault the server messed up, so I turn to leave without saying another word.

"Would you like to place an order to go?" she calls after me.

I don't bother answering. I walk through the double doors to find Doug waiting for me on a bench outside. He smiles up at me as I approach.

"What the hell, Doug? Where were you?"

"I thought we were leaving."

I throw my hands in the air, slowly losing my temper. "What would make you think that? I told you my brother was calling, not that I was ready to go. You didn't say a word to me."

"I'm sorry. Every time Eddie calls, you go running, so I just thought..." He shrugs.

"Well, you thought wrong."

I walk away, toward the parking lot. He catches up with me easily, stopping me and turning me to face him. "Can we not fight?" he says. "I'm sorry, Emmie. Please, it was just a misunderstanding. Let's go to your place and I'll make it up to you." His hands start to move from my shoulders slowly down my back, suggestively. He pulls me closer to him and bends to kiss my neck.

My skin breaks out in gooseflesh as his warm breath brushes over me. "I'm not mad," I say. "Just hungry."

He laughs.

I look up at him. "Eddie is waiting for me at home. He needs to talk."

I watch Doug's smile slowly fall away. His eyes dim. "So, I wasn't wrong."

"Yes, you were. I was going to stay with you and eat first, but now we can just go." I turn away again, but he stops me.

"Hey, not fighting, remember?" He kisses me again. "Your brother needs you right now. He's having a hard time. I understand."

I smile at him, thankful to have him in my life. *How did I get so lucky?* "He's not spending the night," I say, wiggling my eyebrows at him.

We laugh together before getting in the car and heading for our favorite fast-food joint that's on the way home.

ED
THEN

On the way back to my desk, some of my coworkers are grouped in the aisle, having a discussion. They're all sitting in their rolling chairs, talking in whispers, laughing at something. I'm trying not to look but I can't help but notice that Brooke is with them.

I wish I didn't have to walk past them but it's the only way. As I come toward them, they all look at me and grow silent. I look away, face flaming. Almost to my desk, I freeze when someone calls, "Hey Edward!"

I turn back around, unsure who called out. "Hey."

"You walked right by without saying hi." It's Jeremy. I don't know much about him, other than that he seems to have the same personality as Eric. *At least he's not after Brooke.*

"Oh—uh—hi." I give a tight smile then start to turn back around.

"Wait."

A jolt of adrenaline shoots through me. *What do they want?* It's not a normal occurrence for someone to have something to say to me here. *I know they were talking about me.* I turn back to face him again.

"Do you know anything about floors?" Jeremy asks.

My eyebrows furrow. "Floors?"

"Yeah, you know… the thing you walk on."

My lips tighten.

He laughs. "Relax, Edward. I just want your opinion."

The way he says my name makes me cringe. "On?" I ask, glancing from face to face in the group. *They're all just staring.* I feel the heat creeping back up my neck.

"Which do you think looks nicer—dark floors or light?"

The question throws me off. It's so *random*, I'm not sure what to think. The whole group is silent, waiting for my answer. I fumble for a second before saying, "I suppose it depends on the house."

At that, there's an uproar in the group. Someone says, "I told you!"

Someone else says, "See!"

Another says, "Dark, no matter what!"

I didn't realize that the color of floors was such a hot topic. I can't help but smile with relief. It's nice to feel included. *I'm glad I was wrong.*

Jeremy smiles at my answer. "Smart man," he says. Then, "Hey, listen. The wife is picking out some new hardwood for the house. A bunch of us are getting together, gonna kill it all in a day. You wouldn't wanna join us, would you? I'm buying steaks as a thank you."

For a moment, I'm frozen. I stand there, gaping like an idiot fish. *Am I going crazy?* Has Jeremy really just invited me over, or am I losing my mind? "I… I don't know how to install floors," I say.

"Oh, that's no problem! We'll show you everything you need to know."

Is it me, or is his grin a little too wide?

I look around the group again. Brooke's eyes are watching me, along with everyone else's. *Play it cool, Ed.* "Okay, then. I'd love to help out." *What did I just get myself into?*

"Great!" He claps his hands together, seemingly ecstatic. The truth is, I am too. I'm too happy to ask myself *why*. Why would Jeremy, whom I've barely spoken to a handful of times, really invite me over to his home?

Someone's alarm goes off. Everyone checks their watches. "Back to the grind," they moan. I watch everyone roll their chairs back into their respective cubicles before heading back to my own desk.

I put my headset on, and the first call comes through. "Yeah," the caller says. "Why the hell is my bill so high?"

I go through the motions, pulling up their account, discussing the cost of leaving the space heater on all day, along with Christmas lights year-round. It's funny how people assume I know what they have running. I want to scream at them, "I. Do. Not. Know." I have no idea. The only thing I *do* know is how many kilowatts their electric meter is pulling. That's it.

But call after call, it's the same thing. Over and over. People thinking I know the answers. I wish I could tell them all the same thing: "Turn off the damned lights. Turn off the AC. Turn off the TV." Instead, I'm forced to hear complaint after complaint about how *greedy* I am, how *unfeeling,* and all the other *beautiful* names and descriptions they have for me. *Me.* Not the electric company, not the bill. Me.

Brooke stands up and motions for me over the divider. I put the caller on hold and take off my headset. "Brooke?"

"There's someone calling for you."

My eyes widen, shocked. "Who is it?"

"I'm not sure. She asked for you by name, though."

"Okay, let me just finish this call."

"No problem." She smiles at me and sits back down. "Just give me a thumbs up when you're ready."

I get back to my current caller but can't focus like I should. *Who would be asking for me?* Then dread fills me as I think about my mom. *Oh god, not her.* I steel myself, knowing that's who it has to be.

After wrapping things up as quickly as I can, only half aware of what the caller was saying, I give Brooke the signal. The beep comes. It's *Em* on the other line.

What is she thinking? I thought she would get the hint that I'm busy today. I knew I was in for the questioning when she saw me this morning. I don't know how I can explain to her about *him.*

Em has crossed a line this time and it's hard for me to speak with her. My pulse quickens with every word she speaks. *I had it in my head that something happened to you*, she says.

Why does she always jump to the worst conclusions about me? She could give me a little more credit—she *knows* I'm at work today. I can't stand this anymore. I can't take another minute of my family. I need to get them off my back. I need to be free.

EMMIE

THEN

Halfway up the front walk, Doug stops me. He rubs a hand behind his neck like he wants to say something, but he's holding back. "What is it?" I ask.

"I've never met your brother."

I smile. "Are you nervous? You don't have to be."

"It's not that."

"Then, what's wrong?" I'm trying to be patient with him, but my arms are full of bags of food, and the night air is chilly. I want to get inside.

"I think you guys need some alone time right now. I'll take a drive to give you some space."

"What? Doug, No. That's not necessary at all."

He takes a step toward me. "Do you need me to hold that for you?"

I step back. "No. I have it. Don't change the subject."

He sighs. "I don't want the first time I meet Eddie to be when he's going through something and needs you."

"He's always going through something! It's Eddie we're talking about."

"You know what I mean. I don't want to be the third

wheel here. And I really think he's going to feel more comfortable being open if it's just you." Doug leans down to kiss me. "I'm not avoiding this, I promise."

Anger is rising in my chest, but I know he's right. The only way Eddie's going to talk is if we're alone. But Doug doesn't have to leave. He can just make himself busy or something. After all this time together, and him still not meeting anyone in my family, I really do feel like he *is* avoiding them.

I look up at him with thin lips. "If we're going to have a future together, you're going to need to face him eventually."

"I know. Trust me, I know."

"You could come in for a second and we'll eat. Then just make up an excuse and leave."

"No. I think it's better if I just come later. If he's still here when I get back, I'll meet him before he leaves."

"But—"

"Trust me, Emmie. This is for the best."

I nod, not agreeing in the slightest but also not willing to argue about it, then I head for the door. I'm done arguing; I can't make him come inside if he's not ready. Balancing the food in one arm, I use my other hand to stick the key in the front door.

All the lights are off. "Eddie?" I call, flicking on lights one by one.

"Em?"

"Where are you? Why are all the lights off?"

He pops up from the couch. "Sorry, I was just resting."

He gives me a hug and eyes the bags of food. "What's all this? I thought you were at dinner when I called."

I smile, shrugging. "Things changed. I thought you might be hungry after all that overtime. Want some?"

"You are a lifesaver."

Eddie digs into the food like a starving man and I'm glad at the way things turned out tonight. He probably hasn't eaten all day and looking at him, I'm not sure how much food he gets on a regular basis.

"There's a ton here," he says between bites.

"Uh, yeah. I wasn't sure how hungry you would be." The lie sits heavy on my tongue. I can't tell him about Doug without having to explain everything else, and I don't want him to feel guilty for coming to me. I'm glad he's here.

"Why is your cat looking at me like that?"

I look around for Shadow. He's sitting on the floor in front of us, licking his paws. "He's not even looking at you."

Eddie looks at me, mouth half full of food. He looks back at Shadow. Swallows. "Em, he's staring at me."

I laugh. "What are you talking about?"

"Em!"

My eyes widen at his tone. He's definitely not kidding around but I'm not sure why he's freaking out over my cat. I stand up and pull Shadow into my arms. "I'm sorry, Eddie. I'll put him in the other room."

"Wait." He stands up and bends to Shadow's level, coming within a few inches of my cat's face. "Look at those eyes, Em."

I turn Shadow around to look. "Hi handsome," I croon. "What's wrong with his eyes?"

"They're so bright." He squints and backs away.

I laugh again and walk down the hall to drop Shadow on my bed. "Sorry, love. Eddie's being weird tonight."

"I didn't know you weren't a cat person," I say back in the living room.

"There's something about that cat, Em. I'm telling you, he's not right."

I smile, not willing to acknowledge what he's saying. I love my cat; he's not going anywhere. "So, let's talk. What's going on with you?"

"You're referring to this morning, I take it?"

"What the hell was that, Eddie? I've never seen things this bad before between the two of you."

Eddie barks a laugh. "You have no idea. And another thing— What's with the 'Eddie' crap? You know I hate that name. And Mom always calling me *Edward*. Why the hell can't you guys just call me what I want to be called?"

"I'm sorry. I just—I like that name. Emmie and Eddie, kind of has a ring to it, right?" I look at him with hopeful eyes, but he doesn't smile. "You're right, though. Mom is always calling me *Emersyn* and I hate that; I know how you feel. I'm sorry. I'll try harder."

"Thanks."

"So—you say I have no idea. Tell me then. Tell me what I'm missing here, because It kills me to see you this way and be clueless."

He frowns. "See me what way?"

I throw up my hands. "I don't know, Edd—Ed. Depressed, I guess. You're distant. You don't tell me anything. You're working yourself to death and climbing out of windows. Are you afraid of being at home? Because that's the only thing I can think of."

"I don't tell you anything because I'm not a kid. You're my *sister*, Em. I don't have to report back to you." He's starting to get angry now. I can tell he's losing his patience with me. And he still hasn't told me a thing that's going on.

Tears well up in my eyes a little. "We used to be so close."

"Yeah, well that's when we were kids."

"We're not that old."

"We're almost twenty-five."

"So *ancient*." I pout.

He finally cracks a smile. "You don't have to worry about me. I'm fine, I promise. I'm even going to hang out with some work friends next weekend instead of doing another day of overtime."

"Really? That's great, I'm glad to hear that."

"Yeah. Jeremy is putting new floors in, so we're all pitching in to help him."

My eyebrows shoot up at that, but I decide to say nothing. Eddie has enough confidence issues as it is, he doesn't need my comments adding to it. Instead, I ask, "Is Daddy hurting you?"

When he looks away and the blush creeps up his face, I already know the answer. I clench my fists, waiting. He fidgets in his seat, unable to look me in the eyes. "Yes," he finally says. "He's been hurting me for a long time now, Em."

EMMIE

NOW

I'm shaking as I pass through security. The guard doesn't seem to notice. I keep thinking it's going to make me look guilty of something, but I can't help myself. I'm so frightened and nervous to be here—to see Eddie this way.

"He hasn't spoken a word. Maybe you'll have better luck," the guard says when he's done with my inspection.

My eyes widen at the news. I hope he's exaggerating—that Eddie has at least talked to *someone*. Surely he gets visits from a lawyer, doesn't he?

"Wait here," a different guard says after leading me to a visiting area. "He'll be out soon."

I tap my foot with tense energy. Gooseflesh breaks out on my arms, even though it's not cold. I hear whispers from across the room—other people visiting loved ones.

The adrenaline gives me heightened senses that pick up Eddie's steps from down the hall. I sit up ramrod straight to watch him enter the room. I'm so relieved when I see him, I start to cry. I'm so thankful that the guards seem to be kind to him, and he looks like his normal self.

"Don't cry," Eddie says when he sits across from me.

I wipe my face, knowing I can't be helping him much by looking like this. "I'm so sorry. For everything."

"It's over now," he says.

"How are they treating you?"

"Fine."

"The guard told me you haven't been talking to anyone. Is that true?"

He hesitates. "I wanted to wait for you."

I frown. "Why? Edd—Ed, please tell me you've at least talked to a lawyer."

"I've seen one. He had nothing useful to say."

"Nothing useful? How can—"

"They don't understand!" he yells suddenly, making me recoil. "I'm sorry, I just—I don't want to talk about the lawyer."

My fingernails dig into my palms under the table. One thing is clear—he's not going to try. He's not going to fight this or even attempt to defend himself. "I know how much you've been through, but I need you. I need you to try," I say, struggling not to cry.

"I *am* trying."

"How? Please tell me *how* if you won't talk to anyone— won't even speak with your lawyer about it? How are you going to defend yourself?"

Eddie laughs. "I'm not going to defend myself. I'm a murderer. There *is* no defense."

"I don't understand! How can you say that?" I can't fight back the tears anymore. The resignation on his face cuts me to my core. "Please, Eddie."

He watches me cry without saying a word. I've always been able to read him like a book and now I can't. It's frightening believing you know someone and then find out how wrong you were.

I make myself sober up. I have to say what I know he doesn't want to hear. "You don't belong in jail, Eddie."

His eyes widen.

"You need—you need to plead self-defense."

"You can't be serious."

"Of course I am," I say, looking him right in the eyes. "You can do this."

Eddie shakes his head. "Don't you see it's no use? There's too much stacked against me to try playing that game."

"*That game?* Eddie, listen to yourself."

He slams his cuffed hands against the table. "Will you just stop trying to argue with me?" We stare at each other for several heartbeats. Both of us wait for the guard to come over but he's letting us be for now.

"I don't want to argue," Eddie whispers. "All I want is to see you and know that you're okay."

"I'll be okay if you fight for your life. This isn't how it should be. You can't just give up."

He lets out a slow breath and I rush to say, "I want to speak with your attorney. Maybe I can help somehow. I was there—shouldn't he want to talk with me anyway?"

"No. No way. I want you to stay out of this."

"Eddie," I plead. "I need to understand what's going through your head. Why won't you let me help?"

"Just let the lawyer do his job on his own. I don't want you getting dragged into it."

"Can't you see that I'm in it anyway?" Tears of anger pool in my eyes. I'm so frustrated I can hardly see straight. He's not thinking logically about this, and I don't know what to say to make him listen. I'm starting to think there might be nothing at all that will get through his thick skull.

I look at my watch. Our time is almost up. "Even if you won't fight for yourself, I'm going to do it for you," I say.

Eddie presses his lips together. The wheels are turning behind those eyes, but he stays silent.

ED
THEN

Em's eyes are burning like twin fires. She looks like she might spontaneously combust, and I'm worried I've said too much. I reassure myself with the reminder that I can't put her off forever. She's too observant for that. If I'm going to get her off my back, I have to give her *something*.

"What—" She gulps. "What does he do to you?"

"I can't talk about it, Em. Don't you see that?"

"I need to know," she says, her eyes pleading.

I can't tell her. She already pities me so much. I can barely stand the way she looks at me now; if I told her the truth, I don't think I could bear it. "Let's just talk about something else, okay?"

"No, dammit." She slams her fist down on the side table. "There's nothing else to talk about here. You can't keep living there with them. Not like this. How can you stay there with him?"

"I—"

"You what Eddie?"

I glare at her. "I don't have to explain myself to you. I

can't leave, okay? I just can't." Em is crying now. I sigh, hating myself for doing this to her.

"Come live with me," she says.

"No. I can't do that."

"Why not? You're paying Mom and Dad rent, aren't you? Pay me rent instead. You can have the back bedroom. I won't bug you at all, I promise."

This isn't the first time she's offered. Like all the other times, I picture myself living here and struggle with the decision. *What's wrong with me? I should* take her up on the offer. My life would be so much better, so much *happier* if I never had to set eyes on *him* again. But I can't do it.

"Em. We've been over this."

"Why won't you live with me?" My gut wrenches as she wipes the tears from her cheeks.

"I can't do that to you, Em. You have a life. You don't need your brother hanging around like a third wheel. You don't have to babysit me."

"I'm not—"

"Just stop, okay? Just stop asking. You think this is *easy* for me to say no?"

She sniffs and shakes her head.

"*He* sucks, yes. He's... he's a monster, okay? But I'm never home anyway. I'm working on myself and I'm going to get out of there eventually."

"Really?" She brightens somewhat and I give a weak smile.

"Yes. Don't ask me when, just know that I'm working on it."

Em nods. "Okay. Okay, fine, I can live with that. I just want you to be okay."

"I *am* okay."

"Alright, I'm glad." She leans forward and hugs me. I hug her back, glad that this is all settled. Maybe she'll lay off a little now. *I wish my mom was this easy to deal with.*

"You know," Em says. "You can still stay the night any time you want. You don't have to live with me, but you can still get away from them every now and then." She looks straight into my eyes. "I'll always help you. You know that?"

"Thanks. I appreciate that, really. Now, can we talk about something else?"

She bites her lip. "Well… there's something I've been *dying* to tell you, but swear not to tell Mom or Daddy yet, okay?"

I bark a laugh. "Do you really need to ask that?"

She laughs too. "Good point."

"So… spill the beans."

She blushes then, and I have a feeling I know what she's going to say. I clench my fists by my side, preparing myself for the impact. "There's someone I've been seeing."

"Oh?"

She grabs my hands in hers. "Oh, Eddie! Sorry—*Ed*. He's so…" She closes her eyes, searching for the right word. "He's just *amazing*!"

I give a tight smile. "I'm glad you're happy."

"I'm sorry. I know you don't want to hear about my love life, and this is probably the worst time to bring it up. But I want you to meet him."

"Woah, I don't know—"

"You are the most important person in my world, Ed."

My throat tightens. I can't speak, so I nod.

"If you hate him—" She shrugs. "I don't know. I suppose I'll have to think hard about things. I just—I hope you *don't* hate him. I hope you love him as much as I do."

I don't have the heart to turn her down. "Okay. I'll meet the guy."

Em grins. "Thank you. You won't regret it, I promise. I want you to meet him first. Like I said, you're the most important."

I smile, picturing our mom's jealous face when she learns I was the first in our family to meet him. She won't be able to *stand* it. Maybe I'm being childish; most likely, I am.

I picture myself through the eyes of a stranger and that's what I see: a twenty-four-year-old *child*. *His* voice rings through my head, *When are you gonna get that apartment?*

My mom's voice follows. "Edward, are you really wearing *that*? Edward, you didn't tell me you'd be late tonight. Edward, *why* do you treat me this way? Edward—Edward—Edward!"

I cringe, hating what I see. *I'm going to work on myself.* I'm going to change things for the better.

Eddie leaves with a rare smile on his face. Our talk was good, and I'm glad we're on the same page again. I'm glad I can breathe a little sigh of relief now, although he wasn't very clear on what my dad is doing to him. I don't like it, but at least I know Eddie is planning on doing something about it.

I look at the clock, noticing it's getting late. Doug still isn't back yet. I held out a little hope that he would've shown up by now. Eddie and I were talking for a long time. I frown, stifling a yawn, wondering how far Doug drove.

We were supposed to watch a movie together, weren't we? I check my phone for messages from him, but there's nothing. I send him a quick text. **All done.**

He replies almost instantly. **Sorry beautiful, decided to go home for the night.**

Reading those words sends fire through my veins. He's never treated me this way before. How could he just not come back without telling me? I text a heated reply. **What the hell, Doug?**

It's late.

Tomorrow is Sunday.

I'll call you in the morning.

Don't bother. I turn off my phone then, not wanting to see his reply. I'm shaking from anger, and I want to scream. I know I'm overreacting, but I can't get over the fact that he's basically standing me up. And after what happened at the restaurant, it's just too much.

I'm so upset, I think I might actually cry, and I hate myself for being so emotional over this. I hate Doug a little too for making me feel this way over something so trivial. What's at home that's so important to him? He spends the night here so often, sometimes I forget he has a home of his own.

I take deep breaths and plop on the bed by Shadow. He starts purring at my touch, and we lay there together, cuddled side by side, until I fall asleep.

In the morning, I'm disoriented. I yawn and stretch my arms across the bed, expecting to feel Doug's sleeping form. My eyes pop open when all I touch is cold sheets. I see myself sprawled across the bed sideways, then I remember. *He never came back.*

Determined not to let my anger toward him ruin my morning, I get up and go about my normal morning routine. I fill Shadow's bowl with more food, knowing that he'll complain if it's not topped off. I shower and dress, listening to the most upbeat music I can find on the radio.

Once I'm feeling fresh and rejuvenated, I sit down on the couch with a nice cup of steaming coffee. I inhale deeply, letting the aroma overwhelm my senses. I take a sip and sigh.

Next to me on the couch is my phone. I still haven't

turned it on. I look at the black screen, seeing my reflection staring back. I'm not sure if I want to turn it on yet. Maybe I'll leave it off for the day.

Across the room is my bookshelf, waiting for me to pick out the perfect Sunday morning read. I could sit here all day, just sipping my coffee and reading. The thought makes me smile. *Why not?* Why can't I do it? There's nothing else in the world I need to do.

If Doug needs me, he can wait. If my mom needs me, she can wait too. I frown. What about Eddie? If he needs me, I'm not going to make him wait. I look at the bookcase again, calling my name. Then I look down to my phone.

I bite my lip, picturing Eddie trying to call me, trying to get a hold of me. What his face must look like. What if something happened and he needs me? Panic starts to rise in my chest. How long has my phone been off?

I reach for it now, no longer thinking about my mom or Doug. The only thing I can think about is my brother needing me and not being able to reach me. What would he do? Does he have someone else to talk to? I'm not sure if he does.

The screen on my phone turns white. It's agonizing waiting for it to fully turn on. The signal bars at the top are blank. Slowly my signal registers, and the moment it's up, notification after notification flashes across the screen.

My fingers shake as I flip through them one by one, looking for Eddie's name. *He's not here.* I breathe a sigh of relief. *Eddie is fine.* He hasn't tried to contact me. Neither has Doug. But my mom has.

Emersyn, we need to speak, one of her messages says.

Emersyn.

Call your mother.

Why are you avoiding me?

This is urgent.

Message after message, she hounds me. I look at the time stamps, noticing that she hardly waited a minute between texts. There are ten missed calls from her too. *Did she not realize that my phone was off?*

I groan but know the right thing to do is to call her back. My eyes travel back to the last message. *This is urgent.* Something could still be wrong with Eddie. My spine tingles as I imagine him not able to reach the phone.

Without another thought, I call my mom. The phone goes to voice mail. My palms start to sweat. I hang up, dial again. It rings, rings, rings, then voice mail again. "Dammit!" I scream. I wipe my hands against my pant legs, then count to one hundred before dialing again.

"Hello?" my mom's raspy voice greets me.

"Mom, what's the matter?"

"What time is it? What's wrong?"

"What are you talking about?" I demand, growing impatient. "You're the one who blew up my phone. What's the emergency? Who's dying?"

"Oh that." She laughs. "No one is *dying* don't be so dramatic. I thought you were ignoring me, and I wanted to speak with you."

"You said it was urgent," I say, clenching my jaw.

"It was. It is. We need to discuss your behavior and your brother—preferably without you losing your temper."

"I didn't lose my temper with you. I was standing up for Eddie."

"That's not what it seemed like to me," she says. "Anyway, when can you come over again? Or better yet, let's meet for coffee this week. That way your father won't be around to eavesdrop on us."

I run a hand through my hair, thinking. I can't avoid her forever, she's my mom. And I like the idea of my dad not being around. "Okay," I say. "Coffee sounds good. I can meet you on my lunch hour tomorrow, how does that sound?"

"That sounds wonderful. I'll see you then."

I blow out a puff of air. It wasn't as bad as I'd thought. This will be good. We need to clear the air between us.

ED

THEN

A week has passed since Jeremy asked me to come over and help with the floors. I'm standing on his front step now, wiping my sweaty palms on my pant legs, hoping I don't make a fool of myself today. My stomach tightens. I feel sick, but I fight it down.

On a normal weekend, I would be sitting at my desk, about to put my headset on for some overtime hours. Instead of that, I'm now here, ready to *socialize*. I thought about not coming at all. It would be easy to come up with an excuse—a lie to get out of it. I debated with myself all week. I want to yell at myself, *What were you thinking?* But it's too late for any of that now.

I push the doorbell button and wait, trying to clear my dry throat. Seconds tick by. There's laughter inside. *It sounds like there are a lot of people in there. Do I have the right address?* I wipe a bead of sweat from my forehead.

I'm about to press the button again when the door swings open. Jeremy grins at me. "Edward, didn't think you'd show."

"Oh—I can—"

He laughs before opening the door wide. "Come in."

I step into his foyer holding my breath. I wasn't wrong before; there are quite a few people here. I look down at myself, wearing old clothes—suitable for physical work, and back up to everyone else, who seems to *not* be.

Jeremy follows the trail of my gaze. "Looks like you're the only one who came prepared for some work."

"Did I come on the right day?" I ask.

"Yep. We're in back, tearing up the old carpet first. Follow me."

He leads me past the others, who've all grown silent, through to the back of the house. I try not to look at their faces, but I notice a few people from work before looking away. Eric is here. And Brooke. I blush scarlet when our eyes meet, and someone snickers.

Jeremy leads me to a large bonus room that's been emptied out. Tools are piled in the corner, along with stacks of wood flooring. I look down at the carpet that looks brand new. "You can get started in here. Some of the others are going to work on the other rooms," he says. "I'll be in a little later to help out in here."

"Oh… okay."

He pats me on the shoulder. "Thanks, Edward, this means a lot."

"Sure. No problem." I try to smile back at him. "Um— just a question."

"Yeah?"

"I have no idea what I'm doing." I laugh a little, and try to shrug it off casually, but the look he's giving me makes me feel even more stupid.

Jeremy arches an eyebrow. "I thought you said you knew about floors."

"No… I said I *didn't* know how to install them. Remember?"

He sighs. "It's alright. Look." He takes me to the corner, where the edge of the carpet has been lifted. "All you have to do is tear it up starting here." He yanks a little to show me. "See how easy that is?"

"Yeah, looks easy enough."

"That's right. Now once you have it up, there are tac strips that will need to come up." He shows me the narrow strips of wood with sharp tacks poking up from them, that hold the carpet down. "Just use the pry bar and hammer to get those suckers up."

I nod. "Okay. I can do that."

Jeremy smiles. "Atta boy, Edward. I'll be back before you know it."

An hour and a half later, I'm wiping the sweat from my brow as I take up the last strip from the floor. I look around the room, full of pride. *I did it.* I check my watch again. Jeremy still hasn't come back.

My knees crack when I stand up. I wince at the pain, stretching them slowly one at a time. I'll have to ask if he has knee pads to borrow. I'm not sure if I should continue to wait for Jeremy or get started with the wood planks.

I finally decide it's better to go find him rather than screw up his new floor. Stepping out of the room, I expect to hear hammers, or maybe some saws. He said the others were working in the other rooms but all I hear is the sound of people talking.

The smell of something on the barbecue drifts to my nose, making my mouth water. It sounds like everyone is taking a lunch break and forgot to tell me that the food was ready.

I take a step closer to the living room, but stop when I

hear someone say, "My god, Jeremy, how did you get that *loser* to do your floors for free?"

The sound of Jeremy's laugh makes me cringe. "All it takes is a little sweet talk. The man is starved for affection; that much is obvious."

"Do you think he wants to fuck you?"

Jeremy laughs again. "I don't know. Probably. Why else would he be so *helpful*?"

I'm clenching my fists so tightly, I can feel my fingernails cut into my palms. I grind my teeth together, listening to the whole room erupt in laughter. *Brooke is with them,* I remember. My legs feel weak suddenly. I brace myself against the wall.

I feel lost. I don't know if I've ever felt this way my entire life. Even *he* wouldn't pull something like this. At least he would be straightforward with his hatred. Those people out there aren't planning on doing any work at all. They're seriously having a *party* while I'm expected to do this alone.

With careful movements, I turn around and head back to the bonus room. I allow myself to smile. Jeremy wanted me to install his floors. Well, we'll see if he makes the mistake of trying to manipulate me again.

I look at the carefully stacked planks sitting, waiting. One by one, I take a piece and cut it into shorter pieces. I move fast, not measuring, not even trying to make them even. Some I cut into foot-long sections, some into three-inch wide strips. Some, I even decide to get creative and cut diagonally.

When I'm done, the room is covered in sawdust and hundreds of pieces of wood planks, all varying in length and widths. Every single piece has the tongue or associated groove cut. I can't help but grin at my work. *Jeremy is going to just love this.*

Brushing myself off, I stand up and leave the room.

Jeremy is in the living room, just like I thought he would be. He stands up from the couch as I approach. "Edward, done already?"

"Yep, all done. I prepped everything for you. Should be a piece of cake for you to install," I say loudly enough for everyone around to hear.

"Oh, I thought you would stick around—"

"Sorry, something came up. I have to leave." I look around from face to face, looking at the people who were supposed to be helping, the people who *knew* what Jeremy was pulling and said nothing to stop him. Each and every one will be engraved into my memory for a long time. My eyes land on Brooke before I look back to Jeremy.

"We were just taking a little lunch break," he says, still oblivious to the fact that I overheard his conversation.

"No problem. I'm not hungry, thanks for offering though."

He blushes. I smile and pat him on the shoulder. Then I turn and walk out the front door without another word. When I'm pulling away, I can hear the sound of his wife screaming, even with the windows in my car rolled up. I'm not sure if I've ever been this proud of myself in my life.

EMMIE

THEN

I'm alone in my office when there's a light knock at the door. "Come in," I call. I look up from my computer screen and remove my glasses. Doug stands there with a stupid smile on his face.

I put my glasses back on, turn back to my monitor. "You can leave," I say.

"Come on, Emmie. I came in to work early, just to see you."

"That's unfortunate. I wouldn't want you to miss out on any sleep."

"Don't be like that." He takes a step toward my desk and leans down, trying to meet my eyes.

"I'm not being like anything. *You* are the one being like something, Doug. You didn't have to run away like a scared little boy. Eddie isn't going to bite you."

"I know that, dammit. I—"

"It doesn't matter." I take my glasses off for a second time and glare at him. "I don't have time to argue about this. I'm working."

"I want to explain myself, Emmie. I don't want to leave things like this."

"There's nothing to explain."

"It's me," he says. "You don't have to avoid me. We can talk about this. Tell me what you're thinking, what you're feeling. Don't shut me out."

I slam my hands down on my desk, making him jump. "I don't have anything else to say. You left me. That's that."

I ignore the guilt that fills me when I see the hurt look in his eyes. *He's* the one who hurt me. I'm not going to feel sorry for kicking him out of my office. This isn't the time or place for this discussion anyway.

Doug takes a step back. "Okay." He raises his hands in surrender. "Okay, Emmie. I get it. I won't bother you anymore." He turns to leave.

"Wait," I call to him. When he looks back at me with those wide brown eyes my heart flutters. I bite my lip, wanting to be mad at him and still wanting to kiss him before he leaves. "Will you call me tonight?"

He smiles. "Of course."

I nod. "Okay." He leaves and I go back to work. I check the clock, noting that I only have about an hour before I need to meet my mom.

She's sitting on the patio at one of those tables with a large red umbrella providing shade from the sun. I watch her sip from the straw, holding the plastic cup with her painted fingernails. Her oversized sunglasses block her face, so I'm not sure if she sees me or not.

My mom has always had class. She's always appeared completely put together, never a hair out of place. I envy her. Even if it's all a show, and underneath is nothing but chaos, I feel like it must be nice to at least *seem* totally in control.

"Hi Mom," I say, approaching.

"Emerysn, darling." She stands to kiss me on both cheeks.

We hug and I say, "I'm just going to order really quick."

A minute later, I join her with my own coffee and pre-packaged sandwich. "Beautiful day today, isn't it?"

"Mhm," she says, watching me take a bite.

"So…"

"I spoke with your father."

My eyebrows shoot up. "About Eddie?"

"Yes, about *Edward*. He says he didn't realize he was being so hard on him, and he would try to be kinder."

"Did he say what happened between them?"

She shakes her head. "No."

"Did you ask him what he did to make Eddie feel the need to climb out of a window in order to avoid him?"

My mom frowns. "No, Emersyn. I didn't want to rile him up. He got the point; that's all that matters."

I glare at her. "Thank you for at least doing that."

"Now, I want to talk about you. Enough about this business with your father and Edward. How are things in your life?"

"I'm okay. Everything is fine." I smile a little, thinking about Doug. I wanted Eddie to meet him first, but at least he knows about him. I suppose it wouldn't hurt to mention him to my mom. "I'm seeing someone."

She claps her hands. "That's great news. Tell me all about him!"

I can't help but grin at her excitement. "Doug is amazing, Mom. He's so thoughtful and he always showers me with compliments. He calls me *beautiful* and *gorgeous* and so many other nice things."

"As he should!"

"He listens to me and cares about my feelings. I feel like he's the first man in my life that I can actually say that about."

She nods, smiling. "I can't tell you how happy that makes me. Sometimes I feel like your father—well never mind. Where did you meet this Doug? And more importantly, when do I get to meet him?"

I laugh, knowing she was going to go there. "We met at work. He was a new hire."

"Ah. The old lover at work story!" She grins.

"It's not like that," I say, laughing still. "You know human resources meets all the new hires."

"I'm teasing. So, when do I get to meet him?" she asks again.

"I'm not sure. It might be a while yet."

"Emersyn, you know I need to meet the man in my daughter's life," she says, more serious now.

My eyes flash. "He works nights," I say. "His schedule is all wacky. We'll set something up eventually." I don't mention to her that I've already been seeing him—this isn't a new relationship.

I don't know how I've managed to keep Doug from her for so long, but I'm glad that I have. It's nice to have things in my life that my mom doesn't know about. If she would've known about him, I could just imagine the nagging that would've come all this time. She's already practically demanding to see him. *Just like a teenager again.*

"I want to plan a barbecue," my mom says.

"That will be fun."

"It's a birthday party for you and your brother. To celebrate your turning twenty-five." She laughs. "God, I can't believe how old I'm getting."

"You don't have to—" I start, knowing how much Eddie will hate it. He hates every time she tries doing something like this.

"I want to. Don't worry, I know it's more for me than you."

"Does it have to be for our birthday? Can't it be for something else?"

"No. Now stop arguing." She shrugs. "Invite Doug along. It will be the perfect opportunity to meet him."

"Mom."

"What? Why won't that work?"

I pinch my lips into a thin line. "Maybe."

"No. No maybes. What are you hiding?"

"I'm not hiding anything. I just don't want you to force this on him if it doesn't work for his schedule. I know you, Mom. If you invite him to this and he can't make it, you're going to automatically hate him."

"I promise I won't do that," she says in mock surrender.

I eye her with disbelief.

She laughs. "I swear it, Emersyn. Mention the barbecue to him. If he can't make it, then so be it."

I agree, already knowing how things are going to play out.

Walking up to the building where I work, I brace myself for Jeremy to confront me. He doesn't seem like a person who just drops it when he's bested. I'm not someone who's normally confrontational, and the idea of being forced to talk to him again makes me sick to my stomach. I'm sweating like I'm in a sauna, and it's not from the weather.

Somehow, I make it to my desk without seeing him. I start to breathe easier with each moment that passes without him approaching. I had this crazy idea that he would be sitting in my chair with his feet up on my desk, waiting for my arrival.

I smile to myself, ready to start the day. Maybe I read him wrong. He realized what a dick he was being and that's it. His wife probably put her foot down and said enough is enough, after the results of this weekend. *Hell, I might even get an apology out of him.* I almost laugh at the thought. There's *no way* he'd apologize.

Brooke's perfume is in the air. I turn to see her walking down the aisle, and frown at the look on her face. Her eyes have dark purple rims under them, like she hasn't slept.

Her hair hangs in strings around her face, and I can see the large knots she hasn't bothered to brush out.

She looks terrible. There's something wrong. This is the polar opposite of her usual sunny nature, but there's something inside me that's angry with her and glad she looks out of sorts. *She was there. At Jeremy's.* She knew what he was doing and said nothing to warn me. I was humiliated and she didn't even try to stop it.

That's not what a friend does. That's not someone who cares does. It's obvious she doesn't reciprocate my feelings, but it still stings to be treated that way by *her.*

Instead of talking to her, greeting her with a "Good morning, Brooke." I turn my back in her direction, making myself busy until it's time to clock in. I make a note to have IT change my monitor to the other side of my desk. I want to look in the opposite direction—instead of toward Brooke, away from her.

I put my headset on, ready to start the day. Just before the first call comes through, a piece of paper flutters down to my desk, from Brooke's side of the divider. "I'm sorry," it reads. I crumple it up and toss it into the waste can beneath my desk.

The first call comes through, and then the next, and the next. It's the same thing as every day. People complaining about their electric bills *and I'm the bad guy.* I'm in the middle of reviewing an account when my supervisor leans over my shoulder with a note. "We need to talk after this call."

I give him a thumbs up and block myself from receiving additional calls once this caller hangs up. I feel him hovering there over my shoulder, listening to every word I say. He's so close, I can feel his hot breath moving my hair. I cringe, wanting him to back off, not having the words to say so.

Finally, after an eternity, the call ends. I take my headset off and swivel around to see my boss's unfriendly stare. "What's up, Adam?"

"You've had some complaints against you, Edward. We need to speak about your behavior."

My eyebrows furrow. "My behavior?"

"Please come with me to the conference room."

As I follow him there, past the curious eyes that wonder what's going on, I can't help but think that Adam has me confused with someone else. I don't have behavior problems at work. My work ethic is top-notch. I don't call in sick, I don't show up late, and I don't cause any problems. I do everything asked of me with a smile on my face.

He opens the door to the conference room, and as soon as I enter, it hits me what this is all about. Jeremy is sitting there, along with Eric, and several others who were at Jeremy's house over the weekend. *This is a setup.*

I take a seat as far away from them as I can. Adam sits between us. He has a file in front of him. I'm assuming it's on me. Turning toward me first, he says, "Edward, I'm sure you've guessed why you're here."

I clear my throat. "No, not at all. I actually have no idea."

Adam frowns. "There are several witnesses"—he holds a hand to the others on the opposite end of the room —"who claim that you tried to physically attack Jeremy while on company property."

"I what?" My face flames. I knew he would have it out for me, but to go this far? I could lose my job over a lie like this. I look across the room and notice Jeremy's black eye.

Adam arches a brow at my tone. The others whisper among themselves until he clears his throat. "As I said, there are several witnesses. I'm sure you know this is a terminable offense—"

"I didn't—"

"Please let me finish." He scowls. "Because of your

outstanding work history with us, I'm going to allow you a second chance. Jeremy has agreed it will be acceptable to him as well, although we're moving your desk to a different floor to separate you. You will be under close watch, Edward. One more mistake, I don't care how small, and you are gone."

There are a thousand things racing through my mind right now. My thoughts are so jumbled I can barely distinguish one thought from another. I understand why Jeremy would pull this. I can even understand Eric. But the others sitting in this room? Why would they want me to lose my job?

What have I done to any of these people? I try to be civil, kind even. I try to smile and say good morning when I pass. This makes no sense. Jeremy was screwing with *me* first. Why would he do this to me now, after all I did was stand up for myself?

I look back across at Jeremy, who has a smug look of satisfaction on his face. I feel nothing but pure, hot rage toward him. I hope his wife is the one who gave him that black eye for being such an idiot.

I turn to Adam. "May I speak?"

"Please."

"I'm not sure what they said, what *details* they've given, but I ask you this: is there any camera footage? I did not touch Jeremy. I did not even *try* to. I would never do anything like that, especially not on company property. Please, Adam. *Look* at me," I cry, waving a hand over my body. "I'm scrawny. There's no denying it. Look at Jeremy. He has to be twice my size. Do you really think I could hit him and not get my ass kicked in the process?"

Adam works his jaw, thinking. I can see that my words register with him, but it's not enough. "You attacked him where the cameras didn't reach."

"No, I didn't."

He shakes his head. "There's no use denying it, Edward. I don't believe that all these people would come to me with the same story if it wasn't true. Now, you can go back to your desk and pack your things. Your new desk is on the seventh floor."

Adam stands then, and the rest follow him out. It takes me a moment to compose myself before walking back to my desk. I feel everyone's eyes on me as I pack my box with the few belongings I have and carry it to the elevator.

EMMIE

Kate is the one person in my life whose name my mom doesn't try to lengthen. I've never once heard her refer to Kate as "Kathryn," and I wonder what Kate said to her to keep her in line. It might just be her personality. It's big enough; she doesn't need her name to be big too.

"Stop sulking," Kate demands as Eddie walks into the kitchen. She, Mom, and I are all at the table when he walks past.

To anyone else, it looks like he's ignoring her. But I don't miss his flinch when she speaks. "Eddie isn't sulking," I say, trying to come to his defense. "He's just tired from all that hard work he does. Isn't that right?" Looking at him, I'm not sure if I'm maybe making things worse instead of better.

Kate laughs. "Defending your brother, as *always*."

"That's what sisters are for," I say with a tight smile.

Eddie doesn't answer either of us. He walks past again, back to his bedroom. I want to cry looking at him. He looks so depressed and it's always worse somehow with Kate around.

She leans toward me and whispers, "What's eating him *now*?"

I frown, hating her treatment of Eddie. She's always been kind to me, but too hard on my brother. "He's having a hard time at work lately."

"Wasn't that his problem the last time I saw him?"

My mom clears her throat. "If you don't mind, can we get back to planning the barbecue?"

"Of course, Shawna," Kate says. "You know how your son's problems fascinate me. I'd have no drama in my life otherwise."

"Right. Now, about the menu." My mom makes a list with Kate, calculating how much food they think they'll need, the best cuts of meat to get, and the best things to go with them.

She loves to host. Daddy loves to grill. They make a good pair, and their friends and family are all too willing to come eat the food they offer. I wish she wasn't doing this for us. I know Eddie doesn't want it either. Our tradition is to celebrate together in our own way, but there's no arguing with Mom.

I smile at my mom and Kate, with their heads together like teenage girls. I wonder why Mom wanted me here. It looks like they have everything handled. I'm not sure what kind of role she thought I would play, but it's a little boring to sit on the sidelines and be shushed every few minutes by two expert planners. They don't need or want my opinion.

I get up from my chair, ready to find Eddie.

"Where are you going?" my mom asks.

"Bathroom," I lie.

"Be quick. I want you to tell me what you think about these flowers."

I almost laugh, knowing she'll dismiss anything I say about them anyway. I walk softly down the hall to Eddie's bedroom door. After knocking, I wait. I know he's in there, but he doesn't seem to want to see me. I frown. I thought we were good after our talk the other night.

I knock on his door again. "Eddie?" I say at the door.

"It's open."

I twist the door handle and see him there on his bed. He's laying down, facing the wall. "Eddie? What's wrong?" I take a step into his room and shut the door behind me.

"Nothing."

"It doesn't look like nothing. You didn't even say hi to me or Kate."

He scoffs. "*Kate* can go to hell."

I suck in a breath. "What?"

"You heard me."

"I thought you liked her."

Eddie rolls over and glares at me. "You know how she treats me."

"You know that's just how she is. She treats everyone like that."

"Not you."

"Yes, she—"

"Was there something you wanted?" He's being cold toward me. I know he wants to be alone, but I can't let him stew in whatever this is.

"I'm here for you," I say. "No matter how small or stupid you think it is. I want to hear about it."

Eddie rolls back over to face the wall again. He's silent for a while and I'm about to turn to go. The message is clear, but he finally says, "I almost got fired today."

"What? Why?"

"Just a stupid misunderstanding. It's no big deal."

"Eddie." I come to the edge of his bed and sit. "It is obviously a big deal. If there's a misunderstanding, maybe you can clear things up with whoever—"

"Stop." He sits up and grabs my shoulders. "Stop it, okay?"

"Fine," I reply, shocked.

"I tried to explain, Em, don't you get it? Anyway, I'm not fired. It's fine. It's just—it's frustrating."

"I'm sorry."

He lets out a deep breath. "Me too."

"I'm sure you don't want to hear this… but what if you found a new job? Someplace that respects you a little more?"

Eddie laughs. "It's not the place, Em. It's the people. And it doesn't matter where I go. There will always be people who hate me."

"Don't say that." I wipe the tears brimming in my eyes. "No one hates you."

"They do, Em. They either hate me, or they don't see me. I'm invisible to them."

His voice breaks. The anguish in his eyes breaks my heart. This poor man feels so alone, I don't know what I can say to make him feel better. I'm not sure if anything I say will get through all the hurt he's feeling. I reach out and hug him. I hold my brother, wishing I could take away all of his pain, wishing I could take away every bad thing that he's had to go through.

After a minute, I pull back and look at him again. "Have you, you know—have you tried to talk to anyone? About—finding ways to feel better?"

I'm not sure if I'm getting my meaning across, but Eddie looks away, blushing, and I know he understands. Something pounds against his door, making us both jump. The door swings in and our dad is standing there, looking disgusted.

"What are you two doing in here with the door closed?" he demands.

I'm shocked at the look on his face—at *his insinuation.* I'm disgusted, repulsed. I look at Eddie, who's now crimson. He scoots away from me on the bed. I look back at

Daddy, seeing him in a darker light than ever before. "We're talking. That's what brothers and sisters do..."

"I don't want you to close this door again."

"Daddy—"

He walks away without another word. I look back at Eddie. He can't meet my eyes.

"Eddie—"

"Don't," he says. "I think you should just go."

I nod but he doesn't see me. He's already lying back down, facing the wall again. "I love you, Eddie," I say before leaving.

After Kate's and Em's visit, I called in sick for the first time in my life. It feels good to do something out of the ordinary, something nobody would expect of me. I slept in, too, and I'm sure *he* missed me the most this morning.

He probably thought I got up early to avoid him. Especially after what he said in front of Em. *It's always all about him.*

But for me, today is about *me*. I've been humiliated over and over and today, I just need to be alone. I need to be alone in a way that doesn't involve other people.

My sister's words ring in my ears. *Have you, you know—have you tried to talk to anyone? About—finding ways to feel better?*

She's right. I've known it all along. I need to take matters into my own hands in order to make a change. Standing up to Eric, in the break room with Brooke, and then Jeremy with the floors, was like a high.

For the first time in so long, I was able to hold my head up a little higher. I was able to look at myself in the mirror without disgust. I've been able to sleep better at night, not playing things over and over in my mind that I should've said, should've done. It's like now that I've had that high, I want more. I long for it, crave it, *need* it more than anything else in the world.

I think about what I have to do to get that feeling again. There are so many possibilities, so many people that I need to stand up to. I think about my dad, my mom even, and the people at work. Then I think about my sister.

Has she had to stand up to people for her happiness? Probably not. No one has *ever* tried to pick on her. Everyone loves her. My fists clench on their own, thinking about her having a new boyfriend in her life, living like a picture-perfect couple. Before I know it, she's going to be getting married to the guy.

I could laugh at her, acting like she really *cares* what I think of him. Of course she doesn't care. She's screwing the guy, not me. What does it matter what I think of him? He's probably just another prick, just like all the others she's dated her whole life.

When the house is silent, I make my move. I get up and get dressed as fast as I can, just like normal. Every second that ticks by is like torture, as I expect *him* to step out from hiding any minute. I'm out the door and in my car within minutes.

The first thing I do is call my therapist's office. "Do you have an emergency appointment available for today?" I ask.

"Are you in danger of hurting yourself or someone else?" the receptionist asks.

I take a moment before answering. I want to say whatever will get me in, but I don't want her to turn around and call an ambulance on me or anything. "Myself," I finally say.

"Can you be here in an hour?"

"Have you been practicing your breathing exercises?" the therapist asks.

I'm in her office, sitting on an uncomfortable couch across from her. The room is dark, lit by a single lamp and rays of light shining through the narrow slats in the mini blinds. I think the dimness is supposed to make the room relaxing, but it has the opposite effect on me.

"A little," I say.

"You should make a habit of it." She stares at me. I'm not sure if she wants me to say something or not. It's growing pretty awkward. *Why did I come back here again?* I look away, twiddling my thumbs. "Do you want to do them now?" she finally asks.

"Okay." I close my eyes. I picture myself far away, on a secluded island with not another soul around for a hundred miles. I listen to the ocean waves, the swaying of the palm trees. Squawking gulls are overhead. The sun heats my face and I struggle to keep tears from leaking through my eyelashes. *I am OK,* I think, taking a deep breath. I hold it for a moment, and as I release, I think, *Everything is going to be alright.*

"Good. Again."

Tears are pooling in the back of my closed eyelids. I can't tell myself the words. I can't think them. I take a deep breath and exhale slowly, no longer seeing the island but instead seeing a sheet of black.

"How do you feel?" the therapist asks. I don't think she can really see my face, or if she can, maybe she's ignoring the obvious.

"Fine," I say.

"I want you to practice the breathing at least once a day.

Work on changing your negative thoughts into positive ones."

I nod, giving her the response she wants. I have good intentions, but I don't know if I'm going to be able to follow through. I don't know why I bothered coming back. I don't know what I was thinking.

"Do you want to talk about why you're here today?"

I clear my throat. "I—" I hesitate but finally decide that it won't hurt to just say it. "I stuck up for myself for probably the first time in my life. It felt—well, it felt good. And I want to learn how to be able to do it all the time. I normally —can't."

"What happened to make you need to defend yourself?"

"It was at work. There are some guys there who think we're all in high school. For lack of a better word, they're bullies." I blush at the word, feeling childish. I feel like a kid who's tattling on his classmates. What she must think of me, complaining about the other boys who won't include me in their group.

"They were harassing you."

My eyes widen. I'm not sure if she's asking it or saying it. "I don't think so."

"Edward, do you know what harassment is?"

"Of course I do. This is different."

She stares at me. I'm not sure what she sees but I don't like the look in her eyes. "Okay," she says. "What happened after you defended yourself?"

I frown, remembering the chat with Adam. "I got in trouble."

She arches an eyebrow. "Do you want to be more specific?"

"No. It doesn't matter now. What matters is, I need to be able to do this more with other people."

"Who?"

I shake my head. "Does it matter?"

"Sometimes the best course of action is to distance yourself from people who are toxic. Asserting yourself is a skill we should definitely work on, but it's important to recognize the toxicity in relationships and put an end to them when you need to."

"What if I can't do that?"

"You can defend yourself all day long with a toxic person, but at the end of the day, nothing is going to change. Toxic is toxic. A healthy relationship means the other person listens to you asserting yourself and changes their behavior to be more respectful, otherwise you're just wasting your breath. Are you willing to waste your breath on these people? Are they worth the effort?"

I think about what she's saying. I picture myself endlessly trying to stick up for myself against everyone and realize she's right. *He* is never going to change. Jeremy and the others are never going to change. When I told Em to call me what I want to be called, she at least apologized and *said* she would try. She hasn't been perfect, but I can tell she's trying. Everyone else though, they wouldn't give a damn.

"I think you might be right," I say. "It's time to cut some people out of my life. *For good.*"

EMMIE

NOW

I thought it would be hard to get Eddie's public defender to talk to me but turns out he was more than willing to find out anything I know. His office is small and crowded with books and piles of paperwork but somehow, he has a system in place with all the clutter.

"Thank you for seeing me on such short notice," I say as he clears off a chair for me to sit in.

"It's no problem, believe me," he says. "Sadly, we're lacking information on this case and anything you can provide will help your brother—greatly at this point."

"I know he hasn't been talking to you. He doesn't want to defend himself and that's why I'm here. I need to make sure you have everything you need—if not from him, then from me."

He adjusts another stack of papers before saying, "The truth of it is, if your brother doesn't want to defend himself, he can just skip this whole process and plead guilty. There's nothing that says he has to go through any of this."

"But he hasn't done that… has he?"

He shakes his head. "No."

"I want to be frank with you," I say. "I think this should

be a case of self-defense—in fact, if he would've just explained in the first place, I'm sure there wouldn't even be a trial."

The lawyer's face falls into a grim expression. "I had hoped you would be able to provide something conclusive that would prove that. A smoking gun, so to speak. I take it you don't have that for me?"

I sigh. "All I have is my witness testimony. I can swear that I was there, and Eddie is innocent."

He shakes his head. "I'm afraid you don't realize how deep of a mess your brother is in, Ms. Daniels."

"Tell me then. Please talk to me because Eddie won't say anything. I need to know how this is going to play out. I need to do something—to help—"

"I'm sorry, there's only so much I can say. I need his permission to talk to you about the case—but I will say this: his best shot here is going to be pleading not guilty by reason of insanity or temporary insanity."

My eyes grow wide at the words. He wants Eddie to plead *what?* As if reading my thoughts, the lawyer adds, "There are more facts here that you aren't aware of, I'm afraid. I wish I could say more. My advice is to try getting Eddie to speak."

"There's nothing else you can do?"

He shrugs. "I'm sorry."

I leave his office feeling more discouraged than ever. *There has to be another way.* But it's going to be impossible for me to fight this battle alone, without Eddie trying to.

"So… what do you think?" I ask Eddie, visiting again, again trying to get him to see reason.

"Em," he says, warning in his tone.

I hold my hands up. "I'm sorry."

Eddie shakes his head. "No, I'm sorry for being so disagreeable. I know you're trying to help. Just—I wish you would understand."

"How can I possibly when you won't explain?"

Eddie pinches his lips into a fine line.

"You won't think about self-defense," I hedge. "What about going a different route?"

He remains silent, so I push on. "Plead—insanity if you must." I choke on the words, forcing myself to continue. "So they can get you the help you need."

Eddie's wide eyes transform to narrow slits in an instant. It looks like he's thinking very carefully before speaking. "Have *you* talked with my attorney, Em?"

"No, I haven't. I didn't know that was an option." The lie sits heavy on my tongue.

He looks at me with mistrust now and it breaks what's left of my heart. He sees right through the lie. I'm trying to be strong for him but it's the hardest thing I've ever done. I never dreamed I'd be in a situation like this—my *brother* in *jail* for *murder*.

"I don't believe you," Eddie says. "I know you think you know what's best but trust me—you don't."

"Of course I do! Eddie, just think about it, please. I know you don't like that word—*insane*, but just ignore it. Think about the help you'll get, versus being stuck with others who won't understand—who *can't*."

"You think I'm nuts now? What happened to self-defense—that was what? Two seconds ago? Which is it, Em? Crazy or defending myself?" The anger is radiating off of him in waves. I want to reach out and touch his arm, but it feels like there's a whole world of misunderstanding between us.

"I don't think you're crazy," I whisper.

"I need help though, right?"

"What if you do?" I demand, wiping tears from my cheeks, knowing if I don't force this conversation on him, he'll avoid it until it's too late. "What if—what if that's exactly what you need?"

Eddie swallows hard. He blinks at me.

"Time's up," a guard calls.

"Eddie?"

"Don't call me that."

"I'm sorry. Ed—"

He works his jaw like he wants to say something else but can't think of the right words.

"Please think about it."

He nods. "I love you, Em."

"I love you." I rush to hug him, not caring that I'm not allowed. I can't stand the rift between us.

A guard pulls us apart almost the instant I have my arms around him. "No touching."

I watch Eddie as they take him away. "I'll see you tomorrow!" I call to him.

EMMIE

Kate is drunk already, laughing obscenely at something Daddy said. I watch him grin at her, loving the attention. He puts a hand on her shoulder, leans closer, and whispers something. *Isn't he supposed to be grilling?*

I haven't spoken with him since he walked in on me and Eddie. What he said to us was inexcusable and I'm starting to have an idea of how he treats Eddie regularly. My mom has been too busy to talk about it. I don't want to run to her and tattle every time my dad does something he shouldn't, anyway. *Like she would even do anything.* I was expecting him to apologize, though. To me at least, if not Eddie.

My eyes drift back to my mom, who's completely oblivious to the conversation going on between Kate and my dad. She's mingling with some people I don't know, playing hostess. From my spot inside the house, I can see it all through the window.

I think about how many years my mom has been friends with Kate. I think she knew her even before she married Daddy. Kate licks her thumb before rubbing it across my dad's cheek, cleaning him off. It hits me how inappropriate their closeness is. My mom is less than fifty feet from them, but no one blinks an eyelash that they're standing close enough to breathe each other's air.

I lean toward the window, watching him closer. His eyes are shifting all over, never staying put for more than a couple of seconds. "See something interesting?" Doug's voice makes me jump.

I turn around to face him. "Don't scare me like that!"

He laughs and hugs me. "Sorry."

"I thought you weren't going to make it."

"I wanted to surprise you. After you forgave me for being so stupid, I figured I owed this to you. It's for your birthday, after all."

I smile, remembering how we *made up*. "I think this is more important to my mom than me. But I appreciate you being here. Thank you."

Doug kisses me and then looks out the window, where I was watching moments ago. "So, what's so interesting out here?"

"Nothing," I lie. I already told him about my dad and what he said to me and Eddie. I don't want Doug to hate him, and I don't want them to get off on the wrong foot. I turn him toward me, holding his hand. "Are you ready for this?"

"Meeting your entire family for the first time all at once, and in front of all their friends? Umm… yep. No problem. Not nervous at all." He grins at me to show me he's kidding.

"We don't have to do this today. We can do something quieter, more private, another day."

"Nope." He shakes his head. "I'm here now. This is going down. Let me just use the bathroom first. You go ahead, I'll meet you in a few."

I look back out the window as Doug heads down the hall to the bathroom. I look past the sea of people until I find Ed, sitting alone beside the pool. He's looking down into his hands, seeming to talk to himself. He's obviously upset. I think about going to sit next to him but maybe I'll wait a few minutes to give him some time.

Moving from the window, I grab a pitcher of iced tea and head outside toward my mom. She smiles when she sees me, relief in her eyes. "I was just thinking about that," she says.

"I read your mind."

"Ha ha," she says dryly. "Set it there next to the ice."

"You should relax. Everything is fine."

"I am relaxing." She smiles too wide, and I know she's lying. I wonder why she does this to herself over and over every year. Even if not for a birthday, it's always for something. She loves to have these stupid get-togethers but during them, she doesn't get a moment of peace.

"So, does Daddy have the meat ready?" I ask, trying to get her mind to focus on him and what he's up to while she's stressing herself out.

She takes a moment to look around, finally seeing that he's nowhere near the barbecue. She frowns. "Well, I thought he was cooking. I better go grab him."

"Good idea. I'm starving."

My mom is walking away when she turns and says, "I almost forgot. Your man, Doug, is he showing?"

I grin.

"He is?" She claps her hands together, thrilled that she'll get to meet him today.

"He's in the bathroom. I'll bring him to you when he comes outside."

"I can't wait!" She continues toward my dad.

I stand alone for a moment, watching. Kate walks away when my mom reaches them. *Is it me, or is she frowning?* My parents stand together, my mom leaning toward him, I can tell she's trying to keep her voice low. His deeper tone carries though. It's obvious they're arguing.

"You never told me," he says.

She whispers something.

"No, you didn't!" he demands.

"I'm not going to be quiet, Shawna. You pull this shit on me every time."

She says something again, too quiet to make out.

"Fine!" He walks away from her, heading inside to get the meat I suppose.

My mom has her back to me, but I don't miss when she reaches a hand up to brush across her face. My throat feels tight. I bite my lip, hating the picture that I see, hating how he's embarrassing not only her but all of us and seems to have no idea.

"Mm, this looks great," Kate says by my side. I hadn't even realized she was next to me.

"Yeah," I say. "Mom's tea is always delicious."

Kate pours herself a refill, grabs some appetizers, and walks away, holding her cup up to me as if to say "Cheers." I nod to her with a small smile before scanning the yard for Eddie again. He's in the same spot, trees partially blocking him from view, still seemingly talking to himself. I don't want to pry any more than I already have, but I can't resist getting a little closer.

THEN

I sit on a bench beside my parents' pool, all alone, feeling probably the most awkward in recent memory. This is supposed to be a barbecue to celebrate *our* birthday, but as usual, it's more about Em than me. I don't mind. Not really. Feeling awkward isn't an unusual feeling; it's something that I've grown accustomed to, but it doesn't make it any easier.

This is one of my favorite spots in the yard, surrounded by trees, barely visible to anyone else, but at the same time, I still have a clear view of everything and everyone. I look out at the yard, watching all the people that my parents know. All their so-called *friends* — Em and I invited no one.

Not even one of them helps my mom. They're eager enough to crowd around her when she refills the snack table or hold out their cups when she walks around with a pitcher of ice-cold tea. I don't see one of them blink an eye when she struggles under the weight of the appetizer tray or help steady her when she almost trips over the steps coming out of the house.

I wonder if she feels lonely in those moments. I wonder if she feels as invisible as I do almost every second of my existence. *I see her, even if no one else does.* A part of me wants to go to her, to help her, be the good son. But I've been there before; I already know what would happen.

"*Edward*, you're fussing over nothing," she would say. "Gosh, you worry more than a mother hen." She'd say it loudly, making a joke for everyone to laugh at. *Emotional*, she might call me, or *sensitive*. She'd try to make it sound endearing, but really, she'd be doing nothing but mocking me.

I shake my head at the image. I'm an idiot for even thinking of helping her. She's no better than *him*.

"Ed?"

I'm startled by the sound of my name. For a moment, I think I'm back at work, daydreaming again. Brooke is here, looking straight at me. She looks just as shocked as I feel when our eyes meet, but she speaks again. "Can we talk?"

"What are you doing here?" I ask.

Brooke blushes. I didn't mean to be rude, but I think I came across that way. I have no idea how she knows my parents or how she was invited to this get-together. I haven't spoken to her since before the flooring incident at Jeremy's. "If you want me to go—" she starts, turning away.

"No, wait."

She turns back. "I'm so sorry, Ed."

My gut clenches when I see tears in her eyes. I ball my hands into fists, fighting back the anger I feel toward myself, toward everything that brought me to this moment, to be the one making her cry. "You have nothing to be sorry for," I say.

"I do, though." She steps closer. "I didn't know what Jeremy had planned, but I should've known it would be something cruel. He invited us all over for a get-together, said he felt sorry for you, and was going to ask you to join too." Her cheeks flush red. "I should've known," she says again.

My lips tighten. I look away, unable to meet her gaze. "He felt sorry for me. And you went along with that. Why would anyone need to feel sorry for me?"

"I-I—" Brooke blows out a puff of air. "I don't know. He said you were lonely, didn't have any friends, and you're always alone, so I thought maybe he was right."

"Did it never occur to you that people can enjoy being alone? Sometimes being alone is exactly what a person needs."

"I'm sorry, Ed. I never thought—"

"Of course you didn't." I turn back toward her. "Maybe next time you'll think twice about making assumptions." I don't know why I'm so upset with her. She was there, yes, but she said herself she knew nothing about what Jeremy was doing. How could she have known? It's not her fault he's such an asshole and I shouldn't be taking it out on her. She's right here in front of me though, and the easiest person to take my anger out on.

"I'm sorry," I say. "I'm sorry to snap at you. It's just hard being humiliated like that in front of everyone."

"You heard what he said?"

"Yeah, I did."

"If it makes you feel any better, he was pretty embarrassed when he walked into that room and saw the floor."

I smile. "I heard his wife screaming before I drove away."

Brooke laughs. "She was so pissed. She turned around and socked him right in the eye."

I can't help but laugh with her. The picture of Jeremy getting hit by his wife, in front of everyone, is something I wish I could've seen. Then I remember his face when Adam called me into the conference room. "He told Adam that I hit him."

"He what?"

"I almost got fired. He had Eric and some others say they saw me do it."

"It's a lie! I'll tell Adam myself—"

I shake my head. "It doesn't matter. I already tried to explain. Adam doesn't want to listen."

She's quiet now, thinking. I watch her eyebrows furrow before she says, "He didn't show up for work this week."

"Maybe he took off to put the floors in himself."

Brooke looks into my eyes. "Jeremy is always at work. Every day."

"And you know him so well? You know what he would and wouldn't do?"

She frowns. "No, I suppose not."

"I don't want to talk about Jeremy anymore."

"Right. Well, I'll see you later." She walks back through some trees and talks with a couple about my parents' age. She gives the woman a hug, then heads into the house.

I feel more alone now than before she arrived. I think about what she said. *He didn't show up for work this week.* A grin spreads across my face.

I think about joining the others. My stomach rumbles, reminding me I haven't eaten anything yet. I reach into my pocket, pull out the piece of notepaper I stuck in there this morning. Last night I spent hours researching talking points, conversational topics, things to say for small talk. I read through the list for the twentieth time today.

Before I get up, I try the breathing exercise that my therapist recommended. Deep inhale... *lie to myself*.... Deep exhale... *lie to myself*. One more time for good measure.

I stand near the food table, an empty plate in one hand, food already long gone. We're all waiting on the meat, that should've been done. I eye the group of people ten feet away. There are only a few of them there. My feet have a mind of their own, taking me to them before I'm fully ready.

The conversation stops. All eyes turn toward me. "Hi." I smile. Someone gives a weak smile. Someone clears their throat. We stand in a circle, all facing each other. I wait, sweat starting to bead on my forehead. My heartbeat is in my throat as the seconds tick by with nothing but uncomfortable silence.

It's too much to bear. I can't take any more. I turn around and walk away from the group. The second I do, laughter rings out behind me. I clench my fists, listening to their conversation resume without me.

I'm about to join Ed and a group of people when he suddenly turns and walks away. He brushes past me, not seeming to notice that I'm there. My step falters when I see how upset he looks. I should go after him, see if he's okay, but I don't want to embarrass him further.

At the last moment, I continue past the group of people, who are now laughing about something. I mingle with various people walking around the yard, wondering when the damned food is going to finally be ready.

A blood-curdling scream fills the air. Silence falls as everyone looks around, trying to pinpoint what's going on. My eyes land on a woman with bloodshot eyes walking across my parents' lawn, straight toward Eddie.

"You fucking did it!" she screams at him, charging toward him.

Eddie looks like a deer in headlights. He's frozen, with wide eyes, seeming to panic. "I—I don't know what you're talking about," he says. He holds out his hands toward her as if to ward her off, but she keeps going.

"You *killed* him!" the woman wails.

Everyone gasps, myself included. We're all frozen,

watching the drama play out in front of us. I finally break out of my trance when I realize no one is going to put a stop to this.

"Eddie," I say. "Let's go inside. You don't have to listen to this." I walk toward him, determined to intercept him from the madwoman.

"What's going on here?" our mom asks, following behind me.

"I have no idea," Eddie says, looking toward us for help.

"Who are you? You're not welcome here," Mom demands of the woman. I'm surprised, but proud of her for actually saying something.

The woman ignores my mom and me. She won't look away from Eddie with her red-rimmed and wild eyes. It seems she has no idea what she's doing or what she's interrupting. I try to maintain control of my temper, but it's hard seeing Eddie being called out in front of everyone for no reason.

"Jeremy," the woman grounds out. "How could you take him from me?" she screams again, an agonizing, ear-piercing wail that makes me flinch.

I watch Eddie's eyes go wide with recognition at the name. He knows whoever it is she's referring to.

"I didn't touch him," Eddie says. "I swear I didn't."

"This is absolutely unacceptable," my mom says in her most authoritative voice. "I will not stand to have you here making absurd accusations against my son. Leave now, before I call the police and have you removed from my property." Her cheeks are tinged pink, and I can tell I'm not the only one struggling to keep control of my temper.

The woman finally turns to look at her. She looks around, seeing everyone's curious eyes on her. She leaves without another word. Eddie and I both release a breath.

My mom follows the woman to make sure she's actually leaving.

The moment she's gone, everyone starts to murmur in soft tones among themselves. "What was that about?" I whisper to Eddie.

"A guy at work," he says. "That was his wife."

I frown. "Did something happen to him?"

"I don't know." He looks at me, fear still in his eyes. "I don't know why she would say those things to me, Em."

"It's okay, we'll figure this out." I hug him, trying to provide what little comfort I can.

My mom comes back to us. "Where's Doug?" she asks me, like nothing out of the ordinary just happened.

I arch an eyebrow at her. "Aren't you worried about that little scene?"

"Of course I am. But now isn't the time." She looks around, discreetly taking note of everyone's attention still on Eddie. "This isn't how my barbecue is going to end," she hisses at me. *Her barbecue.*

Her meaning is unmistakable. She doesn't want the incident being the talk of the town when everyone leaves in an hour. She doesn't want the embarrassment. I sigh then look around for Doug. He should've come out of the house by now.

He's nowhere to be seen. I check my phone for messages, but there are none. "I'll go look for him inside," I say.

"I'll go with you," Eddie says.

"No. You stay here," my mom says. "If you leave, it will only garner more attention."

I leave them both to look for Doug inside. He's not in the bathroom, nor anywhere else. I go back outside, look for him in every corner of the yard. I go out front, to the cars, look for him there. I grind my teeth together, finally realizing that he's left me again. Just like before.

ED

THEN

I thought I knew humiliation before, but it was nothing compared to this. Jeremy's wife did this to me. My jaw clenches as I think *she deserves every ounce of her misery.*

I'm glad she's suffering. I hope she loses *years* of her life grieving Jeremy, wondering what might've happened to him. I hope she loses sleep every night for the rest of her life.

One thing is certain. I'm not invisible anymore. All eyes were on me the rest of the barbecue, and all are on me now at work. I'm not sure who else Jeremy's wife spoke to, but word seems to have spread like wildfire. She had it in her head that *I*, of all people, did something to her husband.

I feel nauseous. I want to laugh at the same time, at the stupidity of it. I barely knew the man. I interacted with him a handful of times. But somehow, everyone has the quiet loner pinned as a murderer.

Every day that Jeremy doesn't show up for work it gets worse. I want to scream at the top of my lungs. "Does Jeremy really have no one else in his life who hates him?" It's hard for me to believe.

I imagine a slew of people rubbing their hands together

in glee, loving that the attention is on me and not them. I'm the one he had his sights on, his *target*. So that makes me the culprit.

It's disturbing to know that this is how everyone's thoughts travel. It's annoying, isolating. But there's something I tell myself to get me through every day. *They'll never find a shred of evidence.*

They can suspect me until they're blue in the face, but it won't matter. At the end of the day, that's all it will ever be. Suspicion. "Let them think what they want," I remind myself. "It doesn't matter."

At lunchtime, there's nothing I want more than to leave the building and eat my food in my car. I can't do it though. Not yet, at least. If I make myself scarcer than normal, it will make me look even worse than I already do. I try not to care how it will look, but I just don't want any more trouble.

I'm sitting at a table near the window when Brooke joins me. It's the first time since I've known her that she's joined me on her own. She smiles when I look at her, surprised. "Mind if I join you?" she asks.

I shake my head, still chewing my food.

"It's weird not seeing you every day," she says.

"Yeah—it is."

"How do you like your new desk?"

Her cheerful demeanor is a nice change but doing nothing to keep everyone's attention off me. I don't want to give her the cold shoulder. I could never do that to her. "It sucks," I say, making her laugh.

I smile. "Did you expect me to lie?"

Brooke shakes her head. "No, not at all. I guess I just didn't expect you to be so frank about it." She pauses. "I'm going to speak with Adam today. This is so stupid."

"Please don't. I don't need any more attention on me."

"Why's that? Guilty conscience, *champ*?" Eric asks. Brooke and I startle when he approaches our table. He pulls out a chair to sit next to me without asking.

Brooke looks at him in disgust. "You and I both know Ed hasn't done a thing wrong."

Eric is all innocence. He shrugs. "I don't know a thing about Ed." He looks at me with wide, innocent eyes. "Do you have a reason to hold a grudge against Jeremy?" he asks. "A reason to want something to happen to him?"

"Leave him alone, Eric."

"He's a big boy. He can speak for himself. Can't you, champ?"

My eyes dart between them. I'm unsure what to say. I think about the conversation I had with my therapist. *Toxic is toxic.* It doesn't matter what I say to Eric, it's all the same to him. *There is no right answer.*

"I have nothing to say to you," I say.

Eric's eyes narrow. "Why not?"

I take another bite of my lunch, ignoring him. I can feel the anger radiating off him. I hear him grind his jaw. It makes me smile. I look up and see Brooke's eyes shining. She smiles back at me with something that looks like pride. She takes a bite of her lunch, ignoring Eric now too.

"You did something to him, didn't you?" Eric demands, loud enough to make every head, that's not already looking, turn toward our table.

I take another bite.

"Maybe you're the one who did something to Jeremy," Brooke says. The room is silent. I sit with my mouth full of food, unable to finish chewing.

Eric looks around nervously. "That's r—"

"You're the closest one to him, aren't you? The one with easiest access?" she continues. "There's nothing like a good stab in the back, right, Eric?"

My hand moves on its own, rubbing my abdomen as I think about Doug. I can't seem to get any work done today. He's the only thing my mind wants to focus on, which infuriates me.

I think about when we met. He, a new hire, me, his human resources representative. He walked into my office with such confidence that day. "I'm here for the new hire paperwork," he said.

One look at him, and I was all thumbs, fumbling around my office like an idiot. "Oh, sure." I glanced at the clock. "You're a few minutes early."

He grinned at me. "I like to make a good impression. New job and all that."

I didn't know what to make of him. He was the best-looking man I think I've ever seen, and not only that, but his confidence was also like a magnet drawing me in. It didn't matter that I hadn't even officially met the man yet. I knew I had to be careful not to cross the boundary of professionalism because something told me it would be easy to do. Men who had an attitude like Doug's, were dangerous.

"I just have to finish getting everything together," I said, keeping my back to him. I scraped through my files, not finding a single sheet of paper to tell me who this man was. Normally a hiring manager hands me a signed employment contract and I go from there, drawing the rest of the required new hire documentation up, personalized for each individual employee. But in Doug's case, there was nothing. No record.

After a few minutes of searching, I spun on him. The entire time he'd been so silent I almost thought he wasn't there anymore. "Who was your hiring manager?" I asked.

"Leon."

"When was your interview?"

"Yesterday."

I arched an eyebrow. "Leon didn't want you to do a background check?"

"He never mentioned one. He basically hired me on the spot. Look, is there a problem? Do you need to call him or something?"

"No, no, it's okay. Please sit, I just need to print some things off." I motioned for him to sit in one of the two chairs in front of my desk. It wasn't unusual for Leon to forgo the paperwork or proper channels. He was one of the hardest managers to deal with, but lucky for Doug, I knew what to do.

I was out of it that day anyway, too worried about Eddie, too wrapped up in my own thoughts. I was embarrassed to be seen out of sorts by a new employee. I thought he would start his career always having this image of the HR lady who didn't have her shit in order. I *always* had my shit in order when it came to new hires. But not with Doug.

"Ma'am," he said, grabbing my attention.

I looked up at him with questioning eyes.

"This is probably way out of line, but is there any chance I can take you out for a cup of coffee?"

My mouth gaped open like a fish. I felt the heat on my cheeks and throughout my entire body. *Did he just call me ma'am? God, I feel so old now.* "You're right. It's way out of line."

We stared at each other, neither willing to look away. He waited for me to speak with all the patience in the world. "You can buy me a cup," I finally said, unable to resist a moment longer under his gaze.

I thought he was being kind. I thought there was no way he could be interested in me, especially not in a situation like that, and not with me being all thumbs, not with my office looking like a hurricane had struck. But it turned out Doug didn't care about all that.

He *was* interested. I smile now, thinking about how fast life can change. You meet one person, and your entire world turns upside down.

I thought we were going to have a future. He told me over and over, the words I dreamed of. Our future this, our future that. His behavior now speaks louder than any of those empty promises.

I'm not blind. I know there's something going on behind my back. How could I *not* see it? I don't know what it is, but it's breaking me a little every day. How can I continue to have him in my life when he's doing this to me? How can I not? My hand rubs across the little life growing inside. *I can't lose him.*

ED
THEN

Eric is gone. When I come into work, there's an uproar. Instead of everyone sitting at their desks, headsets on, talking to customers, they're standing in the aisle ways, whispering to each other. Even management is involved.

As I step off the elevator, heading toward my new workspace, I notice the commotion and all the blinking red lights on everyone's phone consoles. "Another employee. Can you believe it?" someone says as I pass.

"I know. I wonder if they're connected," their friend replies.

I frown, wondering what in the world is going on. Then I turn on my computer and the first thing I see is a companywide alert.

Two employees are currently unaccounted for.
Jeremy Oak was last seen at work on Tuesday the 23rd, and Eric Hall was last seen on the morning of Monday the 29th.
There is an open investigation as police search for their whereabouts.
At this time, we do not believe employees of All-Star Electric are

being targeted. However, we have increased security measures outside the building and will be hiring additional security for the graveyard shift as an added precaution.
If you have any information, please contact Detective Martinez at 555-0089.

The first thing I do after reading the message is smile. I blink, reading it a second time and then a third, just to make sure I read it correctly. I struggle to keep a passive look on my face, but I can't help it; I feel nothing but *relief.*

For the first time, I'm glad that I'm on a new floor now. If I was at my normal desk, I think everyone's eyes would be on me. Brooke isn't across from me to chat with, but it's a relief to know almost no one around me. There's nothing to do but sit down and clock in like a good employee, so I put my headset on and get to work.

The hours fly by in a blur. Before I know it, it's time to leave for the day. Again, I smile to myself, thinking about what a great day today was. It was probably one of the best days I've ever had at work. I couldn't even let the people calling me an asshole on the other end of the line ruin it for me.

I bound down the front steps of our building, feeling lighter than I've felt in years. At the bottom, Brooke is there waiting. She smiles up at me. "Hey stranger."

"Hey back."

"You're sure in a good mood today."

I feel the tips of my ears turn red. "I'm not the only one."

Brooke grins. "Are you doing anything now?"

I really hope I'm not as red as I feel. I think about how to answer her, not wanting to sound like I don't have a life, but not wanting to sound busy either, *just in case.* "I—um. I was just—" I rub a hand through my hair, and give a small chuckle. "Nope," I finally admit.

She eyes me sideways and bites her bottom lip. "Do you want to go for a walk or something? We can grab a bite to eat if you're hungry."

"Yes." I say it too fast, but I couldn't care less. If I'm dreaming, nobody better wake me up because this is the moment I've been waiting for, for I couldn't say how long. I don't know what made her ask, but I couldn't be more thrilled.

"Are you hungry?" Brooke asks.

"Yeah. Let's grab some food if you don't mind."

"I was hoping you would say that. I'm starved."

EMMIE

THEN

It's been days since we've spoken. I've been telling myself that distance is the best answer, but it feels like a part of myself is missing without him near me. I ask myself if I'm overreacting and I can't help but lean toward "Yes."

Doug hasn't explained himself yet, but I haven't given him the chance. I just don't want to hear another lie out of his mouth. Even if it's not a lie, I don't want to hear it. I *know* he's doing something behind my back. *What* he's doing, or *who*—well, I'm not sure if I really want to hear about that either.

It's not hard to keep myself occupied. After the crazy lady came into the yard accusing Eddie of the most awful things, I've been solely focused on him. My parents blame *him* for *her* ruining *their* barbecue, of course. There's no surprise there. Eddie gets blamed for everything. It doesn't matter that it was in our honor—for our birthday—that he had no control over her showing up like that. None of it matters.

I press the red button on my phone, declining another attempted call from Doug. The bile rises in my throat; this time I can't fight it back down. I scramble out of bed, making it into the bathroom just in time.

I sit there panting over the toilet seat, tears brimming my eyes. *I don't know what to do.* Slowly, I get up from the bathroom floor and crawl back into bed.

My phone stares at me from the night table. "I can't avoid him forever," I tell myself, even though in this moment it's exactly what I want to do. I huff out a breath, my decision made. When Doug calls again, I'll answer.

The moment I've made the decision, it's like he's heard me. I jump back against the headboard when the phone immediately lights up. "Hello?" I reluctantly answer.

"Are you actually speaking to me?" Doug says.

"Don't make me hang up."

"Just give me a chance to explain."

"There's nothing you can say to make me understand. All you had to do was *not* show up in the first place. This crap with you abandoning me without saying a word, the *second* time you've pulled it... Doug, I just can't handle it. I can't handle being lied to. Not by you."

"I'm not going to lie to you, Emmie. I swear I've never lied to you."

"You're seeing someone else, aren't you?" I choke out, feeling nausea rising up again.

"What? No. No, that's not what this is."

"Then what else would explain it? Don't tell me *another* emergency?" I lace the question with sarcasm, hating that we're arguing, hating this entire conversation. *Why did I even answer the phone?* I don't want to be this kind of woman. I don't want our life together to be like this.

"You were right." He pauses before adding, "I got cold feet. I should've never showed up to begin with."

My eyebrows furrow. This definitely doesn't fit the description of the Doug I know. The *confident,* self-assured man who walked into my office and asked me out within minutes of first seeing me. "That makes no sense," I say.

Doug's sigh comes through the speaker. "I finished up in the bathroom," he says. "I was ready, everything fine, a-okay. Then I stood there for a minute, watching everyone in the backyard. It was the same spot you were looking out the window."

"And the mundane barbecue of suburbia scared the shit out of you?"

He laughs. "No. I just thought what if your parents don't like me? I'm at their house, their get-together with all these people they know. Your birthday celebration—it would just be awkward, to say the least. At least if we met over dinner, it would be short and to the point." He huffs a breath. "I don't know, Emmie. I'm sorry. I know it's stupid. I know I should've said something. It's just—it's the truth. I wasn't ready and I blew it."

I say nothing in response. There's a silence that falls between us as we both think. After a minute, I say, "I told you, you didn't have to meet them at the barbecue."

"I know. I know. I should've listened."

"I just don't understand why you would leave without saying a word. You didn't even text me, Doug. With every-thing that was going on there, and then you went missing, I was a wreck."

"Wait a minute. What was going on?"

"Some insane woman that none of us knew, came into the yard screaming at the top of her lungs."

"She what?"

"Yeah. And the worst part was, she was screaming at *Eddie.* She was calling him a murderer, claiming he took her husband from her. It was in front of everyone, Doug. It was —it was *horrible.*" I hold the phone away from my face so Doug can't hear me sniff and wipe my eyes. The sound of him grinding his teeth through the phone is like nails on a chalkboard.

"I'm so sorry," Doug says.

"Never leave me like that again," I say. I hope he understands my meaning, without me saying the words, *I can't keep doing this.*

"Never," he agrees. "I'm so, so sorry Emmie," he says again.

"I need to be able to rely on you. You understand that, don't you, Doug?"

"Of course I do. I promise, I'm going to make it up to you. In fact, I want you to set something up with your parents soon. No more putting it off."

"I'm not sure if my mom is ready to be stood up again."

"Good point. I need to apologize to her too."

"Yes, you do. But not right now. We need to let the air clear a little after what happened. My parents are still wound up over the woman in their yard ruining their afternoon—"

"*Their* afternoon?"

I huff. "You know how it is. Give it some time."

"How long? It's already been a few days."

I purse my lips, playing with the idea. "Maybe another week? I don't know. Let's just see how *we* are first."

"Okay. I get it," he concedes. "I swear Emmie, I'm going to make this up to you. Within a week, you're going to be in love with me again."

I never stopped, I think. *I could never stop.* Out loud I say, "I'm sick. I have to go."

"Need me to bring you anything?"

"No. Thanks."

"It'll be over soon."

"I hope so."

ED

NOW

It's hard not to think about everything, despite not wanting to. I try to focus on when Em will be back. The hours are slow to pass, taking an eternity to tick by. Inside, my mind is a frenzy. I wish my thoughts could be as still as my body.

I don't hold it against her; it's not her fault.

When I'm finally notified about Em's arrival, I smile for the first time since I've been here. My sister and I have always been close—that will never change, not even now. There are walls between us—literal bars—but it doesn't matter. I won't let it.

The guard leads me out to the same table as before. She lights up when she sees me, which makes me feel marginally better. "Thanks for coming," I say.

"Oh, Ed—of course. I'll come visit as long as they'll let me."

I think about her not visiting and my smile falls. How often will I really be able to see her?

"What's wrong?" Em asks.

"Nothing."

"Have you—have you thought about what I asked?"

"There's nothing to think about."

The sight of Em crying guts me. Her face crumbles. She tries to wipe away the tears, but they roll down her cheeks faster than she can catch them. "Why won't you see that they can help you?" she asks.

I don't want to think about it, but for her sake, I do. What will happen if I go down this road. I picture a much different outcome than before. No longer alone in a cell but forced into groups full of sick people and session after session of therapy.

"What if you don't even have to go to trial?" Em says. "Maybe just explaining everything to the DA or to a judge will be enough." Her eyes light up at the thought.

"I'm not sure it will be that easy—"

"At least you can try!"

"Em—"

"Do it for me, Eddie—Ed."

I sigh. She still can't *not* say Eddie. I want to laugh at how hard she's trying, and it makes me smile, despite everything. "You always loved that stupid name."

Em smiles back. "You always hated it."

I nod my agreement and laugh. "Yeah. I still do." I ask, "Why do you want this so much? It changes nothing."

"It does, though. It changes so much. You would be getting help—and getting better. You maybe wouldn't be locked up for the rest of your life—depending on every-thing. I don't know how it works, but I know you shouldn't live the rest of your life not getting the help you need."

The more we talk about it, the more hope grows in her eyes. It's wrong, all wrong. I shouldn't even be considering it, but I can't help wanting to do it for her. I think about the way I'll be living—no longer an inmate, but a *patient*. I don't like it. Not at all. Em is right about one thing though —no one should have to live the rest of their life without getting the help they need.

"Are you still seeing Doug?" I ask.

Em looks at me in surprise. "Yeah—why are you worried about him?"

I shake my head. "I'm not worried, just wondering. So... where is he?"

She frowns at my curiosity. "He's in the car. I know you two don't like each other but he's been by my side. He waited outside yesterday and is out there again today."

I nod, looking closely at Em's features. "You still love him?"

Her brows furrow. "Why wouldn't I? What's this all about, Eddie? You're scaring me."

"I can't be curious? I just want to make sure you're okay, that's all."

"I'm fine. Everything is fine—well, besides this." She waves an arm around us, gesturing to the prison I'm trapped inside.

"Yeah. I get it."

"So... are you going to talk now? Are you going to defend yourself?"

Em is so naive. It's like talking to a teenager who just doesn't get it but still thinks she knows everything. I clench my jaw, trying to control my temper. Then I say, "Yeah. I'll talk to the attorney."

"Yes! Thank you!"

"But—don't get your hopes up. It's not going to be as easy as you envision. Don't think there's going to be a happy ending, Em. I said I'll talk to him. That's all."

She nods. "Okay. I understand."

I don't have the heart to tell her. I *know* I need to. Not just for her sake, but for mine too—before it's too late.

ED

THEN

I feel like I'm outside of my body, looking at myself from someone else's perspective. This is the chance I've wanted, what I've been waiting for for *so long*. It almost feels like I'm dreaming. I can't help but ask myself how it's possible that Brooke wanted to spend time with me, and *outside of work.*

For some reason, I'd never even thought of *her* asking *me.* In all my daydreams, it was me finally getting the nerve to ask her out. I never imagined she would be the one to do it, and now it almost seems too easy, too natural.

Brooke chose a seafood place that overlooks the Puget Sound. It's not fancy but it's nicer than I'm used to, especially since I don't like going to restaurants by myself. As we sit on the patio outside, she's enjoying the view of the water, but I can't stop staring at her.

The water is reflected in her eyes, making her blue seem even bluer. I gulp down some water, trying to casually wipe my damp palms on my pant legs. "I love the view here," she says. "Have you ever been to this place before?"

"No. Have you?"

"A few times. It's close to home, so—" She shrugs.

I nod. I'm terrible at small talk and not only that, I hate it. I don't want to feel awkward with her, I want to feel normal. I want her to *think* I'm normal. "I'm glad it's a nice day and we get to sit outside," I say.

Brooke smiles. "You're cute when you're trying too hard."

I feel myself turn scarlet. "I'm not—"

She laughs. "It's okay, Ed." She reaches across to touch my hand, still on my water glass. "I want to talk to you about—" She looks around. "About *Jeremy* and *Eric,*" she whispers.

My stomach drops. Of course, she wanted to talk about them. Why else would we be sitting here? I want to slap myself for being an idiot. "What about them?" I ask.

"I'm glad they're gone."

"You are? I thought you liked them, or at least Eric."

Brooke shakes her head. "He just wanted to get in my pants. They both did. I hated how they—" Her jaw tightens. "It doesn't matter. I just wanted you to know I'm glad, and I know you are too. It's okay. You're not the only one."

The pain on her face is so transparent it makes me hate both of them all over again. I picture Jeremy's wife and the pain in her eyes when she was yelling at me in my parents' backyard. Did she know about his behavior? "I *am* glad," I admit. "But… they might not be gone for good. They might come back."

"I don't think they will."

"What makes you so sure?"

She smiles. "Just a gut feeling."

After dinner, Brooke picks a park to go to and we find ourselves sitting on a bench overlooking the water. She sighs as we watch the sunset together. "I love this spot."

"It's nice," I say but I haven't noticed anything except the way the sunset makes her hair shine.

"I walk that trail almost every day," she says, pointing to the trailhead not far away.

"It must be nice to have this place so close to home."

She nods. "Yeah, it's my after-work stress relief. I'm so thankful I can get to the trail from home, too, so I don't even have to drive." She looks at me. "Do you want to go for a walk?"

"I'd love to."

She leads the way to the trail, and we walk side by side through the twilight. "I'm glad you're not mad at me," Brooke says.

I squint at her, confused. "What are you talking about? I could never be mad at you."

"For being at Jeremy's that day. You know."

"Oh, that. You already apologized, and besides, it's not your fault he's an asshole."

She stops walking, and before I know it, Brooke is pulling me toward her. In a heartbeat, she's kissing me. I'm shocked, stunned into silence. For a moment I can't breathe, but my body seems to be able to move without much conscious instruction.

I return her kiss, holding her to me, inhaling her scent, absorbing the feel of her to last me a lifetime. If this is the only time, I want to remember it for as long as I live. I run my hands through her hair, down her back. Hers are around my waist, gripping me like a lifeline.

Brooke breaks the kiss, panting. "Do you want to come over?"

"Yes."

She smiles, takes my hand, and leads me the rest of the

way down the path. We walk faster, both eager. I have no doubt I'm more so than her. *Don't screw this up, don't screw this up!*

I feel my phone vibrate in my pocket. I reach to press the button to decline the call. It doesn't matter who it is. Nothing is going to interrupt this moment.

We reach her front door, and my phone is vibrating again. Again, I decline the call. As she sticks the key in the door, I ask, "What about your roommate?"

She turns to me with furrowed brows. "How did you know I had a roommate?"

I blush at her look. "I—You told me." I shrug.

"Oh, I guess I forgot. No, she's not home tonight." She pulls me inside, slamming the door behind us.

EMMIE

I hate being mad at Doug, but I love when we make up. We haven't laid in bed together like this in so long. With him being on a different schedule, it seems like he's always sleeping when I'm working or working when I'm sleeping.

He called in sick last night so that we could be together and spend the day together. It's giving us some much-needed time re-acquainting ourselves with each other. I look across my pillow at his still sleeping form, glad he showed up last night.

When he swore to me that he wouldn't lie, that he'd explain everything from now on, I believed him. "Even if you're doing something stupid, you tell me about it. Don't keep me in the dark again," I said, and he'd agreed. I'm determined to make this work between us. I'm determined to trust him. Just the few days we spent apart was almost too much to bear.

Playing with the little hair sticking up on his arm wakes him up. Doug rolls over, smiling at me through groggy eyes. "Good morning, queen," he says.

I laugh. "Good morning."

He pulls me to him, kissing me until I'm dizzy. "Let's stay in bed all day," he says.

My stomach rumbles. "How about breakfast?" I say.

"I'll cook."

I get up and shower while he takes care of our meal. When I meet him in the kitchen, he's whistling to himself, waiting for me with a grin on his face. "What are you so happy about?" I ask.

"You. Us. Our life together."

His smile is contagious. "I'm happy too."

"When are you going to tell your parents and Eddie?"

I bite my lip, still unsure. "Soon," I say.

"Why are you so hesitant?"

"You know why." I sigh. "I don't want Eddie to take it the wrong way."

"Why are you so worried about your *brother* when it comes to *us*?" The anger in Doug's tone sets me on edge. I don't like when he tries to come between me and Eddie. He, of all people, should understand how much Eddie means to me.

"He's my brother, Doug. I'll always worry about him. I thought you accepted that."

Doug looks away, working his jaw. "I do accept it. It's just—I want you to be happy to share our good news, not worried it might *offend* your brother. You can't tiptoe around his feelings your whole life."

I frown. That's not what I've been doing. Is it? "I don't want to rub my happiness in his face. I'll tell him. And I am happy to share. I just put myself in his shoes and can't help but think it would make me feel pretty shitty if he was rubbing his good fortune in my face all the time."

"It's not all the time."

"He's my brother. He's the most important person in my life." The moment the words are out, I wish I wouldn't have said them. Doug scowls at me, the jealousy radiating off him.

"Is he now?" Doug says through a locked jaw. His reaction startles me and frightens me a little.

"Doug—"

"No. Don't."

"You know what I mean."

"I know you mean *I'm* not as important as *him*."

"He's my brother!"

"Exactly!" he screams.

I take a step back. He takes a step toward me. "I'm sorry. I shouldn't have yelled," he says.

I shake my head, unable to believe this is happening. The man I love is jealous of my brother. How can he not understand? I suppose Eddie and I being so close can be hard to deal with, but why should it be? I want him to love Eddie as much as I do, anyway. If he can't, then we're going to have problems for the rest of our lives.

"Doug, Eddie needs me. I'm the only one he has." I reach for his arm. "But *I* need you. *You* are my person."

He looks down into my eyes, softening slightly but not quite all the way. "I guess being an only child has made it hard for me to empathize with your guys' relationship. I'm sorry," he says.

"I should've been more careful with my words. I didn't mean to hurt you."

"It's okay. I overreacted."

"Let's go back to bed," I say.

Doug kisses me. "I'd love to, but I just remembered, I have to be in early today since I called out last night."

"I don't understand. I thought we were going to spend the whole day together."

"I'm sorry. It totally slipped my mind. Frank covered for me, and I told him I'd cover for him, so I'm going in a few hours early."

I look at the clock on the microwave. "You still have hours."

"By the time I get home, shower, get ready—"

I wiggle my eyebrows. "You can shower here—"

"I'm sorry, Emmie. I have to go." Doug pecks me on the forehead before turning to leave. He leaves me alone, wishing we would've never gotten out of bed. Somehow, I think if we wouldn't have had that little argument, he wouldn't have *remembered* to go into work. I sigh. At least he didn't just disappear this time.

ED
THEN

After the best night of my entire existence, I don't want to go home. I know I can't hang around Brooke's place, so I leave her while she's sleeping. I don't want to see the look in her eyes when she wakes up and sees me still there. The awkwardness that will show when she's trying to figure out a nice way to tell me to get the hell out. I'd rather beat her to it and not make her have to say anything at all.

The only place I can think of going is my sister's. I find myself on Em's front step, listening to her talk to someone inside. I feel embarrassed suddenly for not calling her first to make sure that it was okay. I walk back to my car, where I sit parked, thinking of where to go next. I look at my phone, scrolling through "Things to do in Seattle" on the internet.

A few seconds later, my phone is vibrating. It's Em. "Hello?" I answer.

"Are you working today?" She sounds like she's been crying.

"No. I didn't sign up for the overtime this week."

"Good. Will you come over?"

"I'm actually right outside."

"Oh." She hesitates. "Even better. Come inside."

I hang up, wondering who she was speaking to to make her so upset. A surge of protectiveness swells up in my chest, and for a moment I realize why Em does some of the things she does. My twin is the most important person in my life, and I would kill anyone who hurts her.

Emmie swings the door open and comes down the front steps before I'm even all the way up her walk. She holds me in a bear hug, latching to me like she used to do when we were kids. "I'm so glad you're here," she says in my ear.

"What's wrong? What happened?"

"Nothing. I'm just glad to see you. I missed you."

I hold her at arm's length, looking at her tear-stained cheeks. "Someone hurt you," I say.

She waves me off. "Just a stupid argument with Doug, that's all. I'm so emotional these days, it's my fault, really." Em's cheeks turn pink at my scrutiny. She leads me inside, where she makes us both a cup of coffee before joining me on the couch.

"So, you look happy today," she says. "What's going on with you?"

I smile, making her gasp. Then I can't help but laugh at her reaction. She looks completely shocked.

"Edward Michael! You're smiling and *laughing*! Spill it now!"

"I went out with someone last night. We had a great time."

Em's smile wavers a little before she brightens again.

"That's great, Eddie! I'm so happy for you. I want to hear all about it."

"I don't know… it was just a one-time thing, I think."

"If you both had a great time, why would it only be a one-time thing?"

"If you saw her, Em, you would just know. This woman is the most beautiful creature in existence. She's so smart and patient and just out of my league by a long shot."

Em frowns a little. "You deserve all that and more, Eddie. And she liked you enough to go out once, she might want to again."

"I'm just trying not to get my hopes up, I guess."

Em nods. "Okay. I understand that. Well, I'm glad you had a nice time anyway."

"So… you wanna tell me what you and Doug were arguing about?"

"It was—he's jealous of you."

My eyebrows shoot up. "Me?"

"Yeah. It's dumb, just—that's what it was about. I don't want to talk about it."

Even though it's completely wrong, Em's words make me a little happy. I've never had anyone in my life be *jealous* of me in any way. It's almost absurd enough to make me laugh, but at the same time, it kind of feels good. When I think about it more though, I'm ashamed. It's Em's boyfriend and he shouldn't be jealous of me. I'm her *brother.* What the hell is wrong with him? What the hell is wrong with me to make him feel like that?

ED

THEN

When Monday rolls around, I'm anxious to get to work and see Brooke again. I'm not sure what she'll say, but I hope it's nothing bad. I hope she's not embarrassed about being with me. If I see shame in her eyes, I'm not sure I could bear it.

Once I've clocked in, I take a few calls, sweating with anticipation of break time. *Will I see her in the break room? Will she stay at her desk?* There's only ten minutes to see her, and every one of them is monitored by the computer. If I'm not back to my desk in time, I'm sure Adam will have something to say about it.

The moment I take my headset off, I practically run for the elevators. In the break room, I wait on pins and needles. There's no way to know if she's taking her break at the same time as me, but we're normally pretty close. Part of me wants to stick my head in the women's bathroom to see if she's in there but I think it might be crossing the line.

I tap my foot as I watch the minutes tick by. Five minutes left and she's still not here. I can take my chances waiting or spend two minutes going to find her at her desk.

I take a deep breath, then opt to go find her at her

desk. Without waiting for the elevator this time, I take the staircase two steps at a time. I'm panting by the time I reach my old desk. Brooke is in her cubicle. I frown wondering why she wouldn't have come downstairs.

"Good morning," I say to Brooke, pretending to search my old desk for something. They haven't assigned anyone here yet, so I can get away with searching through all the drawers without invading anyone else's space.

She's eating some crackers, looking at her cell phone. I know she heard me, but she's acting like she didn't. I feel dread rise up as I watch her scroll through her screen, ignoring me. I clear my throat. "Brooke?"

She purses her lips and swivels away from me in her chair. I look around and then glance at the clock. *Two minutes.* I walk into her space and bend on one knee in front of her. Her eyes look so big; I think I've startled her. "Tell me what's wrong," I say, desperate to make things ok between us.

Brooke shakes her head at me with eyes still wide open. "I-I don't—"

"What is it? What did I do?"

She shakes her head again then pulls away from me. With a swift motion, she stands up from her chair and walks away from me down the aisleway. I'm staring after her, when she looks back at me, with something that looks like fear. *What the hell is going on?*

I stand up and follow. Brooke speeds up and practically runs into the ladies' room. I check my watch again. I don't have time for this. Whatever Brooke is doing, I'll have to deal with it later. Maybe she'll be willing to talk to me at lunch. Without waiting another second, I head back to my desk to log back in before I'm late.

Lunchtime rolls around and I weigh my options before going down to the cafeteria. I'm starting to think that Brooke might just need some time. Or maybe she really is ashamed of what we did, and she doesn't have the heart to tell me to leave her alone.

I decide to confront her. If she regrets it, she needs to say so. If she wants me to leave her alone then she needs to ask. I don't know what's going on with her, but the fear I saw in her eyes earlier scares me to death.

She's alone at a table in the middle of the room. As I approach, she looks up at me with wide eyes. The fear is in them again. "I'm not trying to hound you," I say. "I just want to know what's wrong. I'm worried about you."

Brooke looks like she wants to bolt. Her eyes shift all over, avoiding me completely. "Please," I beg. I pull out the chair opposite her and sit down. She jerks back in her chair, ready to get up.

"I don't know what you're talking about," she finally says. "I don't know who you even are."

"What the hell are you talking about?"

"What are *you* talking about? You're acting like we've spoken before," Brooke whisper screams at me.

"Yeah, I would say we have..."

"*No.* We haven't."

I can't tell what she's trying to pull here. I stare into her eyes that seem so serious, so genuinely confused. I blink and shake my head. "Brooke—we spent Friday night together."

"We did *what?*" She looks completely appalled, like she could never in a million years imagine spending time with me. I grit my teeth, willing my emotion to stay out of it.

Before I can say anything else, she says, "I don't know what kind of game this is but I have to go. Please don't bother me again."

Brooke stands up. "No, wait," I call after her. "Please, Brooke, we need to talk."

She doesn't turn around.

EMMIE

THEN

I'm at lunch with a few friends from work when my phone starts ringing nonstop. I try to silence it, but when it keeps going off again and again, I finally look to see that it's Eddie trying to get a hold of me. My pulse increases as I realize there must be some kind of emergency for him to be calling me like this.

I step away from the table to answer. "Edd—what's wrong?"

"Em. I don't know what to do. I don't know who else to call. I'm—oh god, Em, I think I'm going crazy."

"Hang on, slow down a little. What's going on?"

"Dammit, I *don't know!*" he yells.

I hold the phone away from my ear and get some stares from people close by who can hear him screaming through the speaker. "Where are you? Can you meet?"

There's a pause. "I'm at work."

"Can you take the rest of the day off? I'll leave now too."

"Yeah. Yeah, I'll meet you at your place soon."

I end the call and go back to the table, where my colleagues are still eating. After making my excuses and letting my boss know that I'll be gone for the rest of the day, I head home to meet Eddie. He's on my front step by the time I pull into my driveway.

I rush to him, ready to embrace him in a hug but he grabs me first. When he starts crying into my shoulder, I have to hold back my own tears. I've never seen my brother this upset and it's terrifying. "Shh. It's all going to be okay. I'm here for you. I'll do anything to help," I try to soothe.

We stand there for a few minutes until he pulls himself together enough to speak. Eddie wipes his eyes with his arm, then his whole face with his shirt. "I don't know what's happening," he says.

"Okay. Come inside, let's talk about it."

Eddie shakes his head. "No. I can't be inside right now. I feel too sick."

When he says the word *sick*, my own stomach rolls. I've been doing better lately, but it still comes on at the most inconvenient times. "What about a walk then?" I ask.

He looks up at the gray clouds overhead. It looks like it could rain any minute, but he doesn't seem to care about that. "Let's go," he says.

We walk on the sidewalk through my neighborhood. I stay silent, waiting for him to say whatever he needs to say. I can't help but notice the worry lines on his face. He looks like he's aged years in a single day. I *just* saw him, and he looked great. Now, he looks haggard and worn.

"She said—" Eddie starts. He shakes his head, trying to get the words right. "She said we've never spoken before. She said—" He wipes his face. "She asked me to stop *bothering* her." He looks up at the sky with his hands on both cheeks, looking pained.

"Who said—"

"Now she's *gone*, Em." He stops walking and turns to look at me. "She's just—gone." A tear slips out of his eye and down his face.

It breaks my heart to look at him and see him in such agony. "I'm sorry," I say, grabbing hold of his arm.

"I don't know how it happened," he said.

"Is this the woman you went out with the other night?"

"Yes!" Eddie cries suddenly, making me flinch. "It's her, she's the one!"

"Okay, where does she live? I'm sure we can find—"

"No, Em. No." He grips my shoulders. "You don't understand!"

I bite my lip, wanting to help him with all my heart but with each second that passes, I think I'm upsetting him more with my questions. He doesn't seem to be speaking in a way that makes sense and each new thought aggravates him further. He's holding my arm too tightly but I'm afraid if I tell him he's hurting me it's going to make him feel even worse.

I look around, glad that it's the middle of the day, hoping most people aren't at home to hear him raising his voice. Eddie doesn't seem to notice when I turn us around and lead him back toward my front door. "What do you mean, she's gone?" I ask. "How do you know she's not at home?"

"There was another alert," Eddie says, eyes brimming.

I nod my head like I know what he's saying, even though I have no idea what alert he's talking about. "When did you speak with her?"

He takes a steadying breath. "It was on lunch break. Then she walked away and that was it."

"When did the alert come through?"

"When I got back to my desk."

I tilt my head, mentally trying to calculate the time. Something is off here. We're back at my house now and I invite Eddie inside. "Stay the night with me tonight," I say. "Do it for me if not yourself. Just so we can get this straight."

"I can't. I have to do something. I have to—"

"Eddie, we have to be rational about this. Let's figure this out then we can take action."

I'm surprised when he nods in agreement. "Okay," he says. "Just for tonight."

ED
THEN

I'm so thankful for Em. She took me in when I was raving like a lunatic, she calmed me down and listened to me without judging. She's the only one in the world who would do that for me. I wish I could be as good to her as she is to me. I'm so embarrassed at my behavior. Losing control like that.

I play the day over and over in my mind, but no matter how many times I hit repeat, I still seem to be missing a section. "I went to see her at break time, but I only had a few minutes," I say to Em.

She nods for me to continue. "She basically ran away from me."

"Why did you want to see her so bad?"

"I mean, after our night together, I just thought—" I shrug, my face on fire.

"So, then you saw her on lunch, too?"

"Yeah. That's when she told me to leave her alone."

"And nothing else happened?"

"No. I went back upstairs and by then there was another company-wide alert."

"What do you mean, *another?*" she asks, looking more concerned.

"They sent one out when some other guys went missing."

"Wait, Brooke isn't the only one?"

I nod. "Jeremy—his wife is the one who came into Mom and Dad's backyard."

Em nods in recognition.

"And another guy, Jeremy's friend, went missing too."

"Why didn't you say anything about this?" Em asks.

"I mean, it wasn't a big deal really. Those guys were assholes anyway. They deserve whatever they get."

Em's jaw drops open a little at my vehemence. I can't look her in the eyes; I'm too afraid I'll see the same fear that Brooke had in hers. I didn't tell Em about *that* either. She's taking her time, thinking about what to say, but before she's able to speak her phone rings.

She looks at the screen and frowns. "It's Mom." Em looks back up at me like she's expecting me to say something.

"Are you gonna answer it?"

"Do you want me to?"

No. "I don't care."

She sighs. "I may as well, or she'll keep calling." She slides her finger across the screen. "Hi, Mom." Her eyes move back to mine as she mouths a question, but I can't tell what she's saying so I just shrug. A second later, she's turning on speakerphone. I cringe as our mom's voice comes through the speaker.

"Edward, what were you thinking?" Mom says.

"About what?" I try to keep the annoyance out of my tone but I'm sure she can still hear it.

"You haven't checked in with me *again*! I can't count how many times you've pulled this on me lately. I slaved over dinner and lo and behold, you're not even home to enjoy it and I have to track you down like a *child*."

Em cringes at our mom's tone and words, but I'm so used to them, they barely register. Our mom isn't looking for an answer here, not really. She just wants to complain. It's her favorite thing to do and I'm her favorite person to complain to and about.

I wait for her to stop talking, then say, "I'm sorry, mom." It's all she wants to hear usually, and I'll gladly spit it out if it gets her to shut up and leave me alone.

"Don't 'I'm sorry mom' me, Edward. I'm tired of you treating me this way. I can't put up with this emotional abuse anymore."

I almost spit out my water. I take a big gulp before saying, "I didn't mean to hurt you. I had a rough day, and it slipped my mind, that's all."

She's quiet for a minute then says, "Is this about that woman you're seeing?"

My eyes flash to Em's. She's the only one I've told about Brooke and she swore she wouldn't say anything to mom about her. Em's eyes are wide. She shakes her head, not knowing how our mom found out about Brooke either.

"How do you know about her?" I ask.

"What are you saying? Of course I know about her. I know everything." She brushes me off like my words don't make any sense and doesn't seem to realize how *creepy* she's starting to sound. "So, when are you coming home?" she asks.

"He's staying with me tonight, Mom," Em interjects.

"Why on earth would he do that?"

"He told you, he's had a bad day."

"He's a big boy, Emersyn. Let him speak for himself. You're always doing that, you know."

Em gives an exaggerated eye roll at me. I spin my finger

in a circle, motioning for her to wrap this damned call up. I can't take much of our mom without losing my mind.

"Listen, Mom. We're headed out to get dinner. I'm going to let you go now."

"Fine, but I expect to be kept in the loop when you aren't going to be home from now on. Do you hear me, Edward?"

"Yeah, Mom. I'm sorry," I say.

"Love you, Mom, bye!" Em says then hangs up before our mom can get another word in.

"Please, for the love of God, Em, do not do that to me again," I say. I'm half joking but then I see the tears in her eyes and wish I wouldn't have spoken. "Oh, sorry, I didn't—"

"I didn't know she was that bad," Em says.

For a second, I'm taken aback. Em has always heard how they speak to me. But then I think about it, and I realize she hasn't really. She moved out as soon as we turned eighteen, and I've been alone with them ever since. She hasn't heard. Maybe a little, but not really.

I shrug it off. "It's not a big deal."

"Eddie," she says, reaching for me. "I'm so sorry, Eddie."

EMMIE

THEN

If that's how my mom treats Eddie, I *hate* to think about my dad. No wonder he never wants to go home. No wonder he's having such a hard time. I'm sure his life at home isn't helping a thing.

We got off topic when our mom called, and I can tell he's not done talking about this woman he's so worried about. "There could be a mistake," I say. "About your—your friend. Maybe you read the email wrong, or they put down the wrong name."

Eddie shakes his head before I'm done speaking. It's like he doesn't want to listen to rational thinking. "I mean, it just seems really fast to be sending out that kind of alert. Especially if you spoke with her minutes before. Normally there's contact with the police first, right?"

He shrugs. "I don't know how they handle things like that. It's just a company thing, nothing official. Maybe someone noticed her missing from her desk and they couldn't find her—"

"But you said you *just* saw her."

"That's why I said I don't know what the hell is happening!" he screams at me, his face bright red. Tears are leaking out the sides of his eyes. I flinch at his tone, but I understand why he feels so out of touch. It would be worrying to me, too.

"Have you tried calling her?"

He shakes his head.

"Maybe you should."

He thinks about it. I can tell he thinks it's a stupid idea but he's considering it instead of just shooting the idea down. "She asked me to leave her alone," Eddie says.

"Then are you sure that she's not avoiding you? Maybe she left work trying to clear her head or whatever and no one could find her and now all of a sudden everyone thinks she's missing?"

I can see the wheels in his head turning. It makes sense.

"Maybe," Eddie finally concedes.

He needs to do something to get his mind off her. If she's really missing, then someone will call the police and get an investigation going. Eddie might really like this woman, but he has enough on his plate already. I can't let him drive himself crazy over this.

"I think you should call her, leave her a voice mail to let her know you're worried, then forget about it for a few days."

Eddie's eyes go wide. "I can't just—"

"I think you should, Eddie. If you make a big deal out of this, you could scare her. Maybe she just wants to be left alone for a while."

He pinches his lips into a line, then he pulls out his phone. I see him flipping through the screens, then he barks out a laugh. "What is it?" I ask.

"I don't even have her phone number! God, how pathetic am I?" Eddie runs his hands through his hair, laughing at himself, all the while the anguish on his face is heartbreaking.

"Eddie, don't."

"You're right. Let's talk about something else. I need to get her off my mind. In fact, are you hungry? Let's go grab some food."

He drove me to a seafood restaurant on the water. We're sitting outside on the patio now, and he can't stop looking around. His eyes dart from face to face, analyzing everyone in the other tables and anyone who comes through the swinging glass door.

"Do you like this place?" I ask.

"Hm? Oh, yeah, good food."

I nod. "I love the view. Great choice."

My phone starts vibrating, rattling the silverware against the glass tabletop. Eddie is too distracted to notice. I think about ignoring Doug because Eddie needs me to be here for him right now, but I also think how worried I would be if Doug denied one of my calls.

Grabbing my phone, I say, "I just need to take this really quick. It's Doug."

Eddie furrows his brows and nods.

"Hey, Doug. I'm out with Eddie right now," I say after accepting the call.

For a second, he doesn't speak. I look back at my phone to make sure I have a signal. "Doug?"

"Tell him."

"Doug, I'm not—"

"Do it, Emmie. Call me later." He ends the call without saying goodbye. My nerves prickle at his attitude but I can't help but enjoy him bossing me around a little. He's never been demanding with me before.

"Everything okay?" Eddie asks, no longer looking from face to face but looking straight at me.

"Fine. Doug says hi."

Eddie arches an eyebrow at me.

"What?" I ask, growing defensive at the look on his face. "Nothing."

He must've heard. "Eddie, I need to tell you something."

"What is it?"

"I-I wanted you to be the first to know. Because you know how much you mean to me, right?"

He shrugs and says nothing.

"Well… I'm pregnant."

ED

THEN

I'm not sure what game my sister is playing at here, but I'm growing more irritated by the minute. I can't speak, so I glare at her, hoping she can read my thoughts, so I don't have to say them aloud.

"Don't look at me like that," she says.

I look away, toward the water.

"Eddie, don't be angry with me."

"I'm not."

"I can tell that you are."

"Why did you choose this place, Em?" I demand.

Em falls silent, her mouth gapes. "I-I didn't. You did."

"Stop playing games with me, dammit!"

Em's eyes are almost bulging out of her head. She looks around, noticing all the people looking our way but I don't care. "Eddie—"

"Don't *Eddie* me, goddammit Em!"

"I'm sorry—" She sets her jaw. "*Ed*, setting the restaurant aside for a second, even though it was *you* who brought us here—"

I open my mouth to speak, but she holds up a finger, stopping me.

"What does that have to do with what I just told you? You're going to be an uncle."

I grind my teeth together, trying to keep it together. I don't know what's wrong with me today. "You just told me about this guy," I say.

"I've been with him for a while," she admits, blushing. "We both had a lot of things going on and I didn't want to bring it up unless it amounted to something, and I guess it does now." She gives a weak smile.

"Are you worried?"

"Yes—no—I mean, not more than the normal about to be a mom stuff. Is that what you mean?"

I'm having a hard time thinking of something to say to her. She's watching me with those expecting eyes, those *hopeful* eyes. What does she think I'm going to say? "Congratulations," I ground out. Then, "I think when the food comes, we better get it to go."

"Eddie wait. Please."

"I need to use the bathroom. I'll be right back." I push my chair back without looking and ram into a server who's holding a tray of drinks. The tray falls, shattering the glasses, soaking me, the server, and another man sitting nearby.

After the spill, it's so silent I think I can hear my heartbeat in my ears. Every single set of eyes is on me. Even those sitting inside near the window are watching. "I'm so sorry," I whisper to the server, mortified.

Em is the first to stand up. She rushes to help me up, grabs a napkin off the table, and starts trying to dry my face off. Some others nearby stand to help pick up the largest pieces of broken glass. Em whispers something to someone but I'm too ashamed to look anywhere but the floor.

I meet her eyes. She nods to me, and I leave.

It feels like an eternity that I'm waiting for her in the car. I clench my eyes shut, willing the memory of what happened moments ago to stop playing over and over in my head. I slam my palm against the steering wheel, hating myself for not paying more attention, hating myself even more for leaving Em to handle it alone.

It was my mistake; I should be the one in there dealing with it. Why did I just leave her like that? I moan in embarrassment, swearing to myself that if she's had to pay for any damages, I'm going to pay her back with interest.

She's finally walking out, holding a bag of food in one hand, talking on her cell phone in the other. I'm starting to get really curious about this *Doug*. Normally I wouldn't bother but something tells me that I should make more of an effort to meet the guy. Especially since he's going to be the father of my niece or nephew.

EMMIE

NOW

Visiting Eddie in prison is one of the hardest things I think I've ever had to endure. It's up there with watching him be miserable for his entire life, but somehow, it's worse because neither of us had a fighting chance.

It was always going to happen one day—a person can only put up with so much before they break. Why couldn't my parents see that? I wonder if they didn't know what they were doing to him—to both of us, or just didn't care.

Doug gives me a reassuring smile when I get back to the car. "How'd it go?"

"He's going to try now," I say, breaking down in Doug's arms as tears of relief come pouring out of me. He holds me, saying nothing, and when I look up at his face, I'm surprised by what I see there. He's wearing a grim expression.

"Are you sure that's wise?" Doug asks.

"What are you talking about? Of course it's wise. He needs to tell them everything, mount a defense. If the only defense is to plead insanity—well, it's better than nothing at all. Besides, if he needs mental help, he should make sure he gets it."

Doug purses his lips and nods. It's obvious there's something else he wants to say but he remains silent. As I drive us away from Eddie's prison to our normal lives, I can't help but think about my brother's line of questioning.

Why would he be thinking about Doug at all? He has his plate so full of other more important things—I realize maybe there's something about Doug that Eddie knows, and I don't.

"He asked about you," I say, keeping my eyes on the road.

"What did he say?"

"He asked if I still loved you."

Doug is silent before asking, "Why would he ask that?"

"I don't know. I wondered the same thing." I risk a glance at him. "Why don't you two like each other?"

"I don't know. I told you that before. You don't believe me?"

"No—I do. I'm sorry," I lie, still believing there's something he's not telling me. He knows everything about Eddie. I've told him everything that Eddie has ever told me in confidence—foolishly thinking I was just venting, and it wouldn't matter.

Now I can't help but wonder if it's something I shouldn't have done. I should've kept my brother's complaints to myself. Doug didn't need to know anyway.

"What do you think happened to those people from his work?" I ask as we near my house.

"You mean the assholes who liked to pick on him every day?" He shrugs. "Who knows? They're probably buried under your parents' house."

A shudder racks through me at the thought. "You don't think—"

Doug laughs. "No, I don't think. I think he probably

took them somewhere and tied them up though. They could be alive still. Maybe."

"We still don't know it was him."

"After what happened with your parents—I kind of don't doubt it."

I choke back tears. We're almost to my driveway when I say, "Hey, why don't we ever go to your place?"

"Because it's a piece of shit apartment. You know that already." His voice sounds defensive.

I bristle but backtrack a little. "Sorry—I just thought we could try something new. Maybe sleep in your bed instead of mine or something. My house is full of—well, full of memories of Eddie."

I've never really thought about it before—it's never been that big of a deal to me. But now that he's so defensive over it, it's got the hairs on my arms raised. *I don't know if I've ever been to Doug's place.*

We've been together so long—I think I remember a small, shabby apartment, in the bad part of town, but I can't make out the finer details in my memory. I've had to have been there already. I'm sure of it. And it's true what I told him. I want to go somewhere other than home because all I see when I'm there, are Eddie's tortured eyes asking me to help him.

Doug's voice softens. "I know it is. Trust me though, my neighbors suck. They're loud—and nosey. We wouldn't get a moment's peace there—or privacy."

"It would take my mind off him, though—maybe." I try to sound hopeful, but it doesn't seem to matter to him.

"I said no," Doug says, a finality in his voice.

We ride in tense silence the rest of the way to my house. I admonish myself for starting yet another argument that was avoidable.

I don't mind that Eddie left me alone at the restaurant. In fact, I'm glad that he did. I'm glad he felt that he could trust me to handle the situation for him. I'm his sister, it's my job to take care of him, after all, isn't it?

I haven't always been able to take care of Eddie, and when the opportunity presents itself, I'm not going to complain. The waiter was an idiot, anyway, complaining left and right about how much his back hurt and about how the damage was going to be deducted from his pay.

"You're telling me there's never any accidents around here?" I said, disbelieving that he would be so rude to a paying customer.

"Not like this, there sure isn't," he said.

"Well, accidents happen, I'm afraid to say. In fact, if I'm not mistaken, *you* weren't watching where you were going and ran right into my brother's chair." After that, there were no more complaints out of his mouth. We even got free dinner out of the deal.

I wish Eddie wasn't so embarrassed, although if I was in his shoes I probably would be too. He hasn't said another word about the baby. I'm disappointed but not surprised. I think he just has to get used to the idea.

"So, when do I get to meet Doug?" Eddie asks me now that we're back in my kitchen, finally eating.

I look at him, shocked. "I thought you didn't really care if you met him or not."

He shrugs. "I guess if he's the father of your kid I'd better."

"You know, it doesn't mean anything," I say. "I mean, you're still my favorite person. I want you to be a part of my baby's life, Eddie."

Eddie nods. "I know."

"Are you going to be okay with all this going on at work?"

He frowns. "I don't know what's going on. I need to find Brooke, but I also need to find a new job before I get fired."

"Whoa, wait. Why would you get fired?"

"They set me up—told my boss that I *attacked* someone. My boss believed them of course. Said there were too many who claimed they saw it."

"That's why you were so upset the other day."

A nod.

"Who would do that to you?"

"The same men who are now missing."

A silence falls between us as I consider what to say next. Eddie works his jaw. It looks like there's more he wants to say but he doesn't spit it out. "I'll talk to Doug," I say. "He might know someone who's hiring. I wish I could hire you myself, but our company has nepotism rules in place."

"That's okay. I'll find somewhere."

"Doug knows a lot of people. You never know, something might come up."

Eddie blushes. "Thanks, Em."

We finished our dinner and while Eddie spends the

night on the couch, I'm staying up for a while texting Doug in my bedroom. His schedule is hitting me hard tonight. I wish he was here to talk to us about all this and be a friend to Eddie in person.

I know Doug's personality would put my brother at ease, and I can't wait for the two of them to finally hit it off. **Know anyone who's hiring,** I text him.

I might. Why? he responds a few minutes later.

I spend some time explaining what Eddie is going through. I don't think he would mind me telling Doug, at least I hope he wouldn't. I lay there, staring at the ceiling, wishing there was something else I could do for Eddie.

He's going through so much right now; I hate to see him miserable like this. I think about him being at home with our parents and it hits me. Daddy. Eddie's relationship with him is a huge factor of his unhappiness, and if I can do something to help with *that,* I'm sure everything else will work itself out.

Eddie leaves first thing in the morning. He was too eager to get back to work and see if it was all just a terrible nightmare or if the woman he cared for was really missing. I think part of him understands that something isn't right with the picture and he's eager to figure it out. I just hope he's safe. I have my own things to take care of this morning.

ork has always been the place I go to get away from home. It's been a sort of reprieve that pays me, so mostly win-win, even despite the negativity I face every single day. Lately, that hasn't been the case. Although it's still leagues better than home, and I've never really looked forward to going to work, I'm starting to *dread* coming here.

This time, I don't have to even enter the building to know something is going on. In the parking lot, several cop cars are parked out front, and it looks like nearly all the supervisory staff is grouped around them. My chest tightens when I feel their eyes on me as I approach the building.

"Is it okay to go in?" I ask when an officer makes eye contact.

He nods permission without speaking, watching me as I enter the building. I feel like I should say something else but I'm too nervous. It's hard enough just to walk past them.

The first thought through my mind is *Brooke*. There's something going on with her. They found her or there's more information. Or maybe they just want to ask questions so that they can investigate her disappearance. Now I wish I would've spoken to them.

Inside the building, I stop in the lunchroom first to drop my food off in one of the refrigerators. It's a rare day that I'm able to actually make something to eat instead of buying, but I take the chance when I'm able to. Since I was at Em's last night, I didn't have to deal with *him* waiting for me in the kitchen this morning.

When I open the refrigerator, it's empty. On a normal day, it's packed full, to the point that you can barely open the door without someone's lunch falling out. Chills run up my spine at the stark emptiness. I hesitate, unsure if I should leave my food inside, then I finally do.

I check my watch. Hope surges in my chest and I reach for the number four button in the elevator. I have to see if Brooke is at her desk. I swear to myself that I'll leave her alone but there's no way I can just go to my office without checking, *especially* with all the police out front.

As I stand in the elevator, waiting for the doors to close and for it to lift me up, I think about the conversation I had with Em last night. It dawns on me that with Jeremy and Eric gone, there's no one to make false accusations against me. The other *witnesses* may now retract their part of the story.

I reach forward and slap the button for the doors to close, more eager than I ever dreamed I could be to reach the fourth floor.

***

Brooke isn't at her desk. I'm not sure why I thought she would be and now I feel like an idiot. Everyone's eyes are on me as I walk through the aisle way. *They know I'm not supposed to be here.*

I want to search her desk for some kind of clue, *anything* that might give me a hint of what's happening with her. I look over my shoulder and can't help but wonder how many people have mentioned me to the police. Instead of continuing to her desk, I stop abruptly and turn around.

I'm able to breathe a little easier knowing that no one here even remembers my name. If anything, they would give a vague description, but I'd be surprised if anyone even knew that Brooke and I had a connection.

There's still time before I have to clock in, and since I'm on this floor anyway, I decide to stop by Adam's office to make a last attempt to defend myself against Jeremy's lies. "Adam, can we talk?" I ask, knocking at his office door.

The door swings in and a room full of police officers turn to look at me.

"Oh, sorry," I say, backing away.

"Stop," one of them orders.

I freeze, terrified of what they might say.

"Can I help you?" he asks, his eyes boring into me.

"I was just looking for my boss."

"And who's your boss?"

"Adam—Adam Hodge."

"When's the last time you saw Mr. Hodge?"

"I—um—I think it was Friday. Yeah, Friday." I stumble over my words, not sure if "Friday" is even an accurate answer. I'm afraid to be speaking with the police and even more afraid that he already knows who I am. I'm terrified that I'm making myself look even worse than I feel and with his eyes drilling into me I feel like a specimen under a microscope. I can't help but squirm and all I want to do is get the hell out of here.

"Where were you when you last saw him?" the officer asks.

"I'm sorry, is there a problem here? I didn't mean to interrupt. I can come back later." I turn to go, afraid to say anything else.

"Adam Hodge is missing."

I stop and turn back. "He's *what?*" I do probably the stupidest thing I *can* do. I run.

EMMIE

THEN

Iknock on my parents' front door, a drink holder full of coffee in one hand, and balancing a box of donuts. My boss wasn't happy with my phone call this morning telling her I'd be in late, but my promise to stay late appeased her for now.

"Emmie, you've been calling in a lot lately, are you sure everything's okay?" she asked, pretending to be concerned. I'm not stupid though, I saw right through her tone. She's annoyed with me and honestly, I can't blame her. I've been putting my family life before work and it's having an impact.

"I know," I said. "I'm sorry. I promise it's an emergency. As soon as this is all figured out, I can get my head back into work." Lucky for me, my boss is understanding when it comes to *family emergencies*, I've covered for her plenty of times for the same reason.

"Hi baby girl," my dad greets me at the door now. "I didn't know you were stopping by." He opens the door wide for me to enter and takes the drink holder from me. "Wow, this looks great. Your mom isn't up yet, I can go let her know you're here."

I stop him before he leaves the room. "Actually, I just wanted to talk to you."

"Oh?"

When he looks at me with wide, innocent, *fake* eyes, I feel my hands clench on their own. "Daddy, I want to talk about Eddie. And I want to talk about what you said to us the time I was in his room."

The smile falls from his face. We're in the kitchen now and he looks away from me to choose a donut before sitting down. "I suppose you're trying to bribe me with all this?" he says.

"Bribe you? Not at all. Is there something I need to bribe you for?"

"That depends. I don't know what kind of *lies* your brother has been spreading."

His tone makes me grind my teeth. I picture him at the barbecue, so close to Kate, and suddenly I want to ask him about that too. I know I have to tread lightly because if I upset him, he won't be willing to talk. I need to hear from his point of view, exactly what's going on between him and Eddie. "Can we start with what you said to us when I was in his bedroom? Why would you say something like that?" I let the tears well up in my eyes knowing that my dad might be immune to Eddie's pain but he's *not* to mine.

Between the tears, I see that I have him exactly where I want him. The look of guilt on his face is unmistakable. "I don't remember what I said," he says. "Don't cry now." He reaches for my hand and squeezes it.

I sniff and wipe my eyes. "You asked us why we had the door closed."

My dad's eyebrows furrow. "Why is that such a big deal?"

"It's what you implied when you said it. I *know* you know what I'm talking about." I let fresh tears fall onto his hand that's still holding mine. Daddy grimaces, always uncomfortable around crying, especially mine.

"I'm sorry," he says. "I don't have a reason to give you —other than that your brother has a way of royally pissing me off."

"But he—"

"And I don't like the way he looks at you dammit!" He slams his fist on the table, making me flinch. "He's a grown man and he needs to stand on his own two feet."

"Daddy, do you think you could try to be a little nicer to him?"

He blows out a puff of indignant air and I continue before he has a chance to speak. "It's just that every time I see you two together, I feel like you just don't like each other very much and it makes me sad. I think it makes Eddie sad too. I know he just wants for you to like him."

My dad lets go of my hand and stands up. "It's always you two against me, you know that? I'm sick and tired of it. I'm sick and tired of being the bad guy. You're twenty-five years old—when the hell are you two going to grow up?"

I stare at him, slack-jawed, stunned. "I'm not trying to accuse you of anything—"

"The hell you aren't. That's exactly what you're doing here."

"Daddy—"

"I can't listen to any more of this. Tell your brother if he wants to bitch and moan about me, he can grow a sack and do it to my face. He doesn't need to cry to his sister when he doesn't like how *Daddy* treats him."

"That's not—"

The sound of the front door closing makes us both whip our heads around. Eddie is standing there, staring at us. And he looks *mad*.

ED
THEN

"That's right," *he* says, looking at me now. "You got something to add, *champ?*"

I only caught the tail end of their conversation, but it was enough. Em was trying to help, but she doesn't realize how much worse she just made things. My eyes flick to hers. She's silently pleading for my forgiveness, and I can't deny her. Of course she didn't mean to make things worse. It's not her fault she's clueless.

"I didn't mean to interrupt," I say, starting for the hallway.

"What have I told you about walking away from me?" *he* says, freezing me in place.

"Is everything okay?" Em asks. "You're home really early."

"Fine. What about you? You're not at work either."

"Don't worry about her," *he* interjects. "What are *you* doing back here?"

"I—I'm feeling sick. I need to lie down."

He arches an eyebrow. "Playing hooky isn't like you."

"I'm not playing hooky. I'm sick."

"Go lie down, Eddie. I'll bring you some chicken broth,"

Em says. I cringe at her thoughtfulness knowing what's coming next.

He slams his fist down on the table. Em jumps then looks at me with startled eyes. *Is this what he's always like?* she's silently asking. I want to scream, *Yes! Every damn day and you're not helping!*

"You're not going to bring him a thing," *he* grinds out at Em. "If he's sick, he can take care of himself like a *grown man*."

It's a gamble, but I take the risk, turning and heading for my bedroom again. I know how *he'll* seethe, but I don't care right now. I don't think he'll hit me in front of Em anyway. And if he does, at least she'll see him for what he really is.

"Are you walking away from me?" *he* calls after me.

I ignore him and keep walking until I reach my door, heart thundering in my ears. I slam it behind me and twist the lock. He's throwing things now and Em is trying to calm him down. I think it's probably working a little at least. He's always had a softer spot for her.

"What in the hell is going on out here?" Mom says.

I smile to myself. *He* woke her up and she's not going to be happy about it. I can't hear what they're saying now; it's all a bunch of muffled words but the gist is that *he's* been careless this time and the women in our family are finally seeing his true colors.

I lie on my bed with my heart still hammering away inside. I can't believe I actually walked away from him. I *actually* did it. Now that I'm home, I don't even know what I'm really doing here. Why the hell did I run from work? I didn't tell anyone, didn't clock out, didn't even clock in *in* the first place. I left my lunch in the fridge, too.

My mind is reeling. It won't shut up. I tug at my hair and clench my eyes shut. I curl up and face the wall, pleading with myself to stop *thinking*. No matter what I try, it doesn't seem to work. All I can do is think about all the things I'm doing wrong and all the things that are going to happen *because* of them.

"La, la, la," I try to make sound to tune my thoughts out. When the sound of my own voice doesn't work, I pull out my earbuds, ready to crank up some music, but I freeze when a knock comes at the door.

At first, I think it's Em coming to my room to talk. I'm about to tell her to leave me alone, but I realize it's not *my* door that's being knocked on. It's the front door. My eyes go wide, and I open my bedroom door to listen.

"Is this the home of Edward Daniels?" a voice says.

"It is," *he* says. "Can I help you?" the anger and malice have left his voice. He's put his mask back on apparently.

"My name is Detective Martinez. I'm hoping to speak with Edward regarding a missing person's investigation. Is he home?"

I can *hear* the smile in *his* voice when he replies. "Yes, he's here. Come inside and I'll go get him."

The footsteps come down the hall. *He* waits outside my door, but no knock comes. Seconds later, his footsteps recede. I crack the door open in time to hear him say, "He's refusing to open the door. Do you want me to take you back there?"

There's a split second, where it dawns on me that this is the worst possible situation to be in. If *he* has his way, I'll wind up in jail and he'll never have to look at me again. I swing my door open and meet the officer in the living room. "Sorry, I was in the bathroom. Detective Martinez, was it?" I extend a hand to shake and don't miss the glare coming from *him* out of the corner of my eye.

"Would you mind giving us a minute to speak in private?" Detective Martinez asks, looking straight at Daddy. I think he sees straight through his lie. I hope so anyway, for Eddie's sake.

"What's this all about?" Mom interjects, annoyed to be excluded from anything involving Eddie.

"Mom, please," Eddie says.

"As I said, there's an ongoing investigation and I'd like to ask your son a few questions."

"Is he in trouble?" Mom asks, eyebrows raised.

"That remains to be seen."

"Let's go outside," I say to my parents, grabbing the coffee and donuts off the table. I lead the way to the back door. They hesitate, eager to find out what's going on with Eddie, but they finally give in and follow me out.

Out back, my mom squirms. I can see how anxious she is, how much she's *dying* to hear what's being said inside. My dad is too. There's an evil gleam in his eye that I've never noticed before.

After today, I realize that there's no more talking to him

about Eddie. It's not a possibility. Whatever is between them, I may never know. But what I *do* know is that Eddie needs to find a new place to live, and fast.

"What do you think is happening?" Mom says.

"It's obvious, isn't it?" Daddy answers. "He should be at work and he's not. Evidently he's done something."

"Maybe he was really sick, like he said," I say. I don't mention the missing people that Eddie told me about. If he hasn't told our parents, then they don't need to hear about it from me.

"I don't believe it," Daddy says.

When they continue to speculate and make the worst kind of assumptions about Eddie, I've had enough. I walk away, around the back side of the house, not wanting to hear any more. I can't believe they won't give him the benefit of the doubt.

"Where are you going, Emersyn?" my mom calls after me.

"I'll be right back," I say. I don't want them to know what I'm doing because they'll give me away. I make my way around the back and side of the house to the side gate. Carefully, I unlatch it and peek around to the front of the house.

When it's clear there're no other police officers out front, I creep behind the bushes under the front windows. There's just enough room for me to squeeze between them and the house. I move slow, staying quiet so they won't hear me from inside. I crawl until I'm close enough to hear almost every word they're saying inside.

"When's the last time you spoke with her?" the detective asks.

Eddie's reply is faint. "I'm not sure. Maybe a week ago now, maybe a week and a half."

"Do you know the date?"

"I can check my calendar. My parents were having a barbecue that day—for my sister's and my birthday. There were a ton of people here who saw."

I realize it's not someone from Eddie's work that they're looking for. It's the woman who was yelling and screaming at Eddie, in the middle of the yard. The detective doesn't seem very suspicious, but I've never spoken with a police detective before. He could have a thousand ideas about Eddie right now and not be giving a hint as to what they are.

A few more questions come and then, "Thank you for your time," the detective finally says. *Crap,* I scoot backward as fast as I can before the door swings open. When the detective's footsteps head down the cement path toward the street, I let out a breath. The door clicks shut, and I wait for the sound of the car to drive away before I make my way back into the backyard.

Our parents are hounding Eddie before I'm able to make it back inside. They heard the car too, it seems. "What was that all about?" Mom cries at Eddie.

"Nothing, Mom. Everything is fine. Please don't worry about it."

"Are you going to just let him talk to you that way, Shawna?"

"Daddy, can I get your help?" I say, walking through the back door just in time. *I* don't even know what I need his help with, but my outburst distracted him at least.

He turns to me while our mom peppers Eddie with more questions. "What the hell happened?" he asks.

"What?" I touch my face, pat my hair and feel the leaves still sticking out on the top of my head.

"You look like you jumped in a pile of leaves."

"Can you help me get them out of my hair?" Tears well up in my eyes. "I fell."

It's not much, but it works. For the next few minutes, he's focused on me and not Eddie. Eddie's eyes meet mine. He understands what I'm doing. *Thank you,* his eyes say.

ED

THEN

Between my family all talking at once, my parents grilling me, this police detective now questioning me, and thought after thought running through my head, my brain feels like it's running a mile a minute. I'm reeling, barely able to put together a sentence to satisfy my mom, and all I want to do is be alone so I can *think*.

When Emmie gets *his* attention, our mom is relentless, hounding me until I finally walk away from her. "I have to go, Mom, I'm sorry."

"What do you mean, you have to go?"

"I just—I just have to think. I need to be alone." I start to walk away from her, toward the hallway and my bedroom door.

She rushes after me and grabs my arm. "You're not going to avoid me!" she cries.

I'm startled. I've never seen her look at me like this—a look so *vicious* in her eyes. I look past her to make sure *he* is still busy with Em. He is, so I yank free of Mom. I say nothing else to her, and instead of continuing to my bedroom, where I know she'll keep hounding me, I leave through the front door.

The bench is empty, so I lay down across its entire length, relieved to be free. I know when I go back the questions will start again but maybe they'll have enough time to at least calm down a little.

I didn't do anything, I tell myself. And it's true. At least, I *think* it is. There are questions swarming like a hive of bees, jumbling together so that they're not entirely clear. Looking up at the dark gray clouds overhead, I wish for rain to come down and wash me away.

I think of this as *our* bench now. It was mine, but then Brooke was here with me, overlooking the water and the sunset, and now images of her here with me flash before my eyes. I think about walking down the trail, just to feel her presence, but I know where it leads, and I don't think that's a good idea right now.

What happened to her? What happened to *them?* I couldn't care less, really, except for Brooke. I can't help but think about how confused she looked the last time we spoke. She acted like she didn't know me. Why would she do something like that?

When my thoughts naturally move to the night we spent together, there's a blank in my memory. I remember waking up and leaving her house... but that's it. I was naked and had to get dressed. Brooke—she was there... wasn't she? I close my eyes to focus but all I see is a wall of black.

Anger and frustration start to fill me up, making me shake. I pound my fists against my head. I *need* to focus! I go back to less than an hour ago when Detective Martinez was asking me questions. He wasn't asking about anyone at work, although I thought that's what he was there for initially.

He wanted to know about Jeremy's wife. "I don't know her," I told him. "Sure, I saw her before—she was ranting and raving in the backyard." I probably saw her at Jeremy's house too but don't remember for sure.

"What happened with you and her husband? Why would she make those kinds of accusations against you?" the detective asked.

"Her husband played a prank on me. It was—hurtful. I don't know why she thinks I had anything to do with him going missing."

He wrote something on a little notepad he carried. I tried to casually wipe my palms on my pants without him noticing, but I'm sure he couldn't miss the beads of sweat on my forehead. He was looking at me with eyes so intent, they seemed to see right into my soul. I was sure he could see everything I've ever done or will do.

Then he was gone. And I'm left asking myself again, why he asked no questions about the people at work. I'm not sure if the lack of interest on his part makes me more worried or not.

Mom rushes over to Daddy and pulls him away from me before I can stop her. "He's gone!" she cries. "He just left!"

"Did he say anything?" Daddy asks.

"No! He refuses to tell me what the hell is going on. Oh my god, Larry." She runs her hands through her hair and staggers backward. "What if our son is guilty of—of —*murder*?"

"Hold on now, who said anything about that? We don't know what the police wanted until Edward gives us some answers. The detective said something about a missing person, that's all. Don't work yourself into a fit."

She glowers at him. "A *fit*?"

He blushes. "You know what I mean." He turns to me, pointing a finger in my face. "And *you*. I know what you did, here."

"I didn't do anything."

"Don't be a lying bitch."

My mouth falls open. He's never spoken to me that way. I'm not sure if the worst part is him saying it so casually or my mom acting like she hasn't heard. The blood rushes to my head and I feel dizzy with adrenaline and anger. "I'm not Eddie," I say. "He may let you get away with treating him that way, but I won't." I stare at him, unblinking. "I'm leaving."

They let me go without apologizing or trying to stop me. Inside my car I brush a stray tear from my cheek, wondering what the hell has gotten into my parents.

Since I'm working late to make up for missing half the day, I'm able to see Doug. He takes his first break in my office, where he holds me while I cry. "You can't let him talk to you that way, Emmie," he whispers in my ear.

"I didn't," I say, wiping my face on his arm. "I told him not to."

"You have to be firmer or he's going to walk all over you. That's how he is."

His words make me feel indignant—he wasn't there, he has no idea. He's never even met my parents, so how would he know *how they are?* But I don't want to start a fight. I nod and lay against his chest while he strokes my hair.

"So, what are you going to do about your brother?" Doug asks.

"I don't know."

"That's not good enough, Emmie."

I look up at him, brows knit. "You were just angry with me for caring too much. Now you're telling me to be more involved?"

Doug sighs. "I wasn't angry. I was—I don't know what I was. But I know you can't stand by and do nothing. He needs you."

"I wanted to help him get a new job. Have you heard of any openings?"

He shakes his head. "That's not going to matter when it comes to your parents."

"It's a start."

"Maybe." His lips thin and he stops rubbing his hands over my hair.

I back away from him, growing angrier but trying to fight the feeling down. "What do you want me to do?" I ask.

"I have to go back to work." Doug turns to leave my office.

"Doug."

He does a half turn. "Yeah?"

"We're not fighting."

"No. We're not." He gives a small smile then leaves.

ED
THEN

I can't go back home. Not with the way things are. I can't rely on Em to take care of me, either. I'm tired of running to her every time something goes wrong with our parents. All I want is to be left alone.

I go to the only place I can think of—a hotel. It feels weird checking in with no baggage. I don't travel often, so being in this kind of environment is odd for me, but it's also a breath of fresh air.

"How many nights?" the receptionist asks when I ask for a room.

"I—um, I'm not really sure."

She gives me an annoyed look.

"Sorry. Um, two—is there one for two nights available?" I hope it's long enough for them to let out a little steam before I come home.

The receptionist's eyes dart across the computer screen. She makes a few clicks and then asks me for payment. Her movements are practiced—robotic-like.

"There's breakfast in the morning at seven, downstairs in the conference room. The elevator is here," she says, pointing to a brochure with a map of the hotel. "The Wi-Fi password is here." She circles a code at the top of the page. "Thanks for staying with us."

She leaves the brochure on the counter, turns around and walks away into an *employee-only* room. Her abrupt departure stuns me for a second. My jaw sags a little but I'm not sure what else I would've said anyway. I head for the elevator.

I decide the best thing to do is take a nap. I can't believe what a relief it is to have this *peace*. It makes me want to consider Em's offer to move in with her again. I know I can't take her up on it—I could never put her out like that. But having a taste of the freedom makes me wish I could. Sometimes I think living with my parents is driving me a little nuts.

Lying on the bed, staring at the ceiling, I take deep breaths, practicing the exercises that my therapist discussed. They help a little—better than nothing at all. My eyes start to droop and within minutes, I'm asleep.

Rapping on the door wakes me. It's loud, insistent. I'm worried that I did something wrong at check-in, and now they're coming to either kick me out or get more money, so I roll off the bed and rush to open it.

"Edward! There you are!" my mom cries when she sees me.

She and *him* brush past me into the room. I stand staring at the hallway, shocked, a feeling of doom overwhelms me. "How did you know where I was?" I finally ask, closing the door.

"Did you forget I have access to your credit card?"

"Since when?" That's news to me. I would *never* add my mom to any of my accounts.

She shrugs. "I don't remember."

"You know why we're here, Edward. Don't turn this into something it's not," *he* chimes in.

I clench my fists and try the deep breathing. It's one of the hardest things I have to do in life—maintain my calm around them. "I can't tell you what the police wanted. They asked me about the woman at the barbecue—that was it. I know *nothing* else."

My parents look at each other. My mom turns back to me. "You have to know something else. You were in there with him for fifteen minutes. What did he ask?"

"Why are you so worried about it?" I ask her, more defiant than before. I'm getting sick and tired of her treating me like I'm still a kid.

"Watch your tone," *he* says.

I shake my head and walk to the door. "Please leave. Both of you." I say a silent prayer. It's the boldest move I've made in my entire life. They both stand there with gaping mouths, staring at me. It's like they can't come to terms with the reality before their eyes.

Instead of listening to me, my mom says, "What *on earth* has gotten into you, Edward?"

Her tone is more than I can take. *He* is probably thinking of various ways to flay me alive, but I don't care. I can't take it anymore. "Get out!" I scream at them. "Get out *now*! Before I call the police and have them remove you."

My eyes move violently between the two of them, glaring at each. I'm panting now, my heart is about to burst from my chest. I feel light-headed as I wait for either of them to make a move.

"Come on, Larry," my mom finally says.

They leave without another word.

EMMIE

THEN

I stand in front of the mirror with my shirt lifted, examining my stomach, attempting to see signs of the life inside. I twist and turn, trying to see if I've grown bigger yet but it's still too soon, I think. I make a mental note to set up a prenatal appointment as soon as possible. With all that's been going on, it's been on the back burner and I'm not going to let it be anymore.

As I'm staring at myself, I can't help but wonder if everything is going to work out. It seems like Doug and I are fighting so much lately—even though we never call it that, and it's starting to worry me. Our child deserves better than a rocky start. I don't like the way my thoughts are leading—I won't let it get to that point.

"We're *fine*," I tell myself, staring into my own eyes through the mirror. I say it again and again until I believe it. "I love him too much to make this not work. It's just all those hormones between us, making me too emotional about every little thing."

When I look down at myself, then back into the mirror, it dawns on me that I've had the wrong attitude all along.

The worry is gone in an instant. What replaces it is a cold determination. "I am *going* to make this work."

No more arguing. No more questioning everything I don't understand. I'm going to be more agreeable. All the little arguments, disagreements—what are they for? Nothing. "I can't lose him."

I set myself an alarm to wake up when Doug is off work for the night. It's early morning, but I want to do something special for him—something to show him how much I love him and to say sorry for everything we've been going through lately.

"There's a surprise here for you. Come over when you're off," I text him a few minutes after my alarm wakes me up.

"On my way," he responds almost instantly, adding an excited emoji.

When Doug steps through the door, I'm waiting— naked. He smiles, almost looking relieved, and the sight of his dimples lights a fire within me. He pulls me close to kiss me.

I pull away from him and drop to my knees, right there in the entryway. I yank his pants down and pull him to me. We spend the rest of the night tangled up in each other.

When I wake up for work, Doug is gone. I force myself not to be frustrated—he does this all the time after all. He usually sleeps better in his own bed, and I can't hold that against him. Most people do, don't they? No big deal.

As I'm pouring a thermos full of coffee, I get a text from him. "Good morning, beautiful. Have a perfect day." The smile it puts on my face stays on me the whole way to work.

When I finally have a minute to myself to think again, it finally hits me how to help Eddie. I don't know why I haven't thought of it before—it's so obvious. I'm going to find those missing people—or if not them, then whoever's responsible for their disappearance.

Yes, it's in police hands, but there's no reason I can't do a little digging of my own. Eddie's my brother after all—if they think he had something to do with a person going missing, I need to show them they're wrong. They shouldn't even be asking him questions in the first place.

"Time to do some research," I say to myself, pulling up the search engine on my computer.

Does All-Star Electric allow the public to enter its facilities?

Various answers populate the screen. One stands out... *call centers are private buildings*. That means it won't be easy to speak with anyone from Eddie's work. It won't stop me though. I can wait outside if I have to.

I type my next search into the bar.

Where is All-Star Electric?

A few addresses come up, none of them for the call center. I try again.

Where is the All-Star Electric call center?

The same addresses come up. Nothing is listed for an All-Star Electric call center. I tap my fingers on the keyboard, frustrated. *Think, Think, Think.*

I know how to get around this. All I have to do is wait outside my parents' house and follow Eddie to work.

My court-appointed attorney sits across from me once again, looking irritated—like I'm the biggest waste of his time he's ever seen. Seeing how I've treated him so far, I can't really blame him, but it still stings. "Are you finally ready to talk to me?" he asks.

"I am."

"Good. Now, tell me what happened."

I explain everything to him—all the gory details, everything down to the bloodstains on my clothes. As I talk, his eyes grow from narrow slits, wider and wider until by the end of my story, they're nearly bulging out of his head.

"Why didn't you say anything sooner?" he asks. There's finally a spark in him. He's ready to get going on the case now that he has some footing.

"I just had to make sure she was okay."

"You should be worried about your *own* ass right now, Edward. You're facing life without parole, here. Information like this is extremely useful for your defense."

"There's no proof, though."

"You leave that part up to me."

"I thought you said there was no defense. You said—"

"Don't worry about what I said. Worry about what I'm saying now that you're actually speaking." He gives me a look that says I should know this already.

"You think they'll let me go?"

He frowns. "No."

"Somehow, I didn't think so." I sigh. "Self-defense?" I ask, already knowing what he's going to say, only asking for Em's sake.

"No—no, I don't think so. There's no chance for that. But I think we have a good shot at not guilty by reason of insanity. We might be able to go with temporary insanity but that's going to be even harder to prove. I'll have to look into it more."

"But I just—"

"It doesn't matter," he says, glaring at me now. "It doesn't matter." He huffs a breath. "You don't want life without parole, Edward. That's the worst possible scenario. You practically admitted your guilt to the police already, not in so many words—thank God—but it doesn't look good. Only one percent of pleas are not guilty due to reason of insanity—and of those one percent, around a quarter are actually successful. We have a long road ahead still, and it's information like you gave me today that we need in our corner."

He still doesn't understand. I grind my teeth together, listening to him drone on and on, when all I want to do is get out of here and go back to my bunk. It was a mistake telling him the truth. He won't be able to help.

"You'll be evaluated," my attorney is saying. "A full mental health assessment will need to be done as soon as possible. I'll notify the court and get everything going." He stands and reaches a hand to shake mine. "I'll be in touch as soon as possible."

To my surprise, it's not long before I'm transferred. My attorney is really doing what he said he would do. Instead of being held on remand at a state prison, I'm now moved to a state psychiatric care facility for the criminally insane—pending mental evaluation.

When they first told me, it sounded like the most frightening place imaginable—worse than any kind of jail or detention center. It didn't take me long to realize it wasn't worse at all. I have yet to meet the doctor, though.

"When will I get evaluated?" I ask the orderly leading me to my new room.

"You're scheduled to see Dr. Reymore this evening," he says. "A nurse will come get you when it's time."

He leaves me alone after showing me around a little. The door is locked for now—*for my own safety*. While I'm alone, I think about what I'll say to the doctor. I practice the words over and over, analyzing how they'll sound and if he'll believe me. My attorney seems to think I'm believable, which makes me feel more optimistic.

I know the conversation can go one of two ways—he either believes me and helps me, or he doesn't. The question I keep asking myself though, is *do I want him to help?* I shake my head at myself. It's too late to go back now. I'm here. This is happening.

"It's a pleasure to meet you, Edward. I'm Dr. Reymore," my new doctor says, gesturing for me to take a seat across from him. He looks at ease—doesn't seem to be worried at all about me harming him. It would be easy to do—if I wanted to. But it's a relief to have his comfort with me seem so natural rather than forced.

"I've looked over your file, but I'd like to hear from you directly. Do you want to tell me what you remember about the day you were arrested?"

I swallow the lump in my throat. *This is my chance.* I can't second guess myself. *This is for the best.*

"My sister has this boyfriend…" I say.

ED
THEN

Sometimes when I wake up in an unfamiliar location, I momentarily forget where I am and how I wound up there. I feel a bigger bed beneath me. I sit up, seeing the large room around me—definitely not my bedroom. I look at the night table beside me and see the pen with the hotel's name written on it. And I remember why I'm here.

I flop back in bed, debating what I'm going to do. I could go to work—I *should* go to work. But I can't help the dread that comes when I think about facing those stares again.

Maybe no one will even notice me. It could be true—they usually don't notice me after all. I'd be surprised if anyone even knew my name. "I'll look even more guilty if I avoid going," I say aloud, forcing myself to hear the words. *I can't look more guilty.*

Then I think about the therapist I saw twice before. *I could take the day off, go back tomorrow with a doctor's note.* I laugh at myself. A doctor's note—from a *therapist*? That will really make me look good, won't it?

"I didn't do anything to anyone," I say.

I force myself out of bed. In the bathroom, I repeat the words aloud, slowly, watching the way my lips form them, taking in every syllable. "I. Didn't. Do. Anything. To. Anyone."

My eyes dart up, no longer analyzing my mouth in the mirror, but my face as a whole. How do I look when I say I'm innocent? Do I look like I mean it? I repeat the words again, watching how my nose flares slightly, my eyebrows tilt. I can't tell if I look guilty or not.

I move to get dressed. *I have to go to work,* I remind myself again. As I clean up and put clothes on for the day, I think about the woman—Jeremy's wife. I can't remember if I saw her at their home or not, that day I went over there.

It's a struggle to remember, but the more I think about it, the surer I am that I didn't see her. *She may have seen me, though.* With the others from work, there are obvious links to me. Jeremy, Eric, Adam, *Brooke*—my gut clenches.

"She's fine," I say. "She's just—on vacation or something. Didn't tell anyone." Hearing the words aloud instead of in my head makes me feel slightly better. "There's nothing I can do about it now."

Am I really going to do nothing about this? "Yes," I say, answering the unspoken question. "There's nothing I *can* do, remember?"

What I *do* remember is the sight of her face the last time we spoke. She had no idea why I was even talking to her. I can't get it out of my head—haven't been able to since it happened. We spent the night together—does that count for anything?

For some people, I know it wouldn't. That's fine for them, but I *know* Brooke. I know there was something there between us, no matter how small. There was no reason for her to act like that with me—like she didn't even *know* me.

Telling me to leave her alone is one thing, but this is different. And now I'm what? Going to just let her be gone forever and hope for the best? "There's nothing you can do, Ed!" I yell it now, as loud as I dare. I say it again and again, drilling the words into myself.

"There is nothing you can do, Ed!"

I look around the room, desperate for something to help me release the pain. There's a pen—that's it. I pick it up, stare at it, and imagine stabbing it into my thigh. *How long would I bleed? How much would it hurt?*

An image flashes before me of my leg dripping blood down my pants. It runs beneath, trailing over my sock, pooling on and in my shoe.

"Stop," I say. I shake my head, hating myself. *God, what a shitty day already.* I set the pen back on the night table to finish getting ready for the day.

Eddie isn't here. The moment I pull up to the curb, I see that his car is gone. "Shit." I slam my hand against the steering wheel. I thought I was being smart waking up early just to get over here and wait for him to leave, but lo and behold, I was wrong.

I bring out my phone to text Eddie and see all the missed calls and texts from Mom. I swipe the alerts off the screen, feeling proud of myself for being able to do it without feeling guilty. Eddie is my primary focus right now —not mom.

What time do you start work? I text him, not wanting to be obvious about my intentions.

While I wait for a response, I get a message from Doug. **Why aren't you at work?**

Color rises to my face. I text back, **Took the day off. How did you know.**

I came to see you. You aren't at home, either. Where are you?

I'm filled with guilt, thinking about Doug waking up early with only a few hours of sleep, just to come surprise me. Thinking about what my boss must think about him going to see me makes me cringe. I'm probably so close to getting fired already—this isn't going to help.

I'm trying to find Eddie, I text Doug back.

A response from Eddie comes through. **Start @ 9. Y?**

I check the clock on my dash. It's 8:15—plenty of time still. "Want to meet for coffee?" I ask.

Doug is calling me now. I slide the screen to answer. "Hey handsome."

"Why are you trying to find your brother? What happened?"

I'm taken a little by surprise at his tone. He's always so kind, always greets me with compliments—never like this. He sounds almost *hostile.* "Nothing happened," I say. "I'm trying to figure out where he works."

"You're going to lose your job if you keep pulling this shit."

My eyes squint. I pull the phone away from my ear to look at the screen, thinking it's someone else who's called me and there's some kind of mix-up. No—no mix-up. It's Doug.

"I know—" I start.

"You don't know Emmie. You should've seen your boss's face when I asked where you were."

"Okay… why are you so worried about it?"

Doug huffs a breath. "I'm just trying to look out for you."

My phone buzzes. "Hang on," I say to Doug. I turn the screen to see Eddie's response.

"Sure. Meet me here—" He gives me the address of a coffee shop and I grin at my success.

I put the phone back to my ear. "Sorry, Doug. I was just reading a message from Eddie. I have to go now—meeting him for coffee."

"Wait a minute," he says, forceful now. "What the hell are you doing, Emmie? And don't tell me nothing. No lies, remember?"

"I—" I pause, hating how he's speaking to me. It's so different from his usual self, I'm thrown off-kilter. What he's saying is right, though. No more lies between us. "I need to find out where Eddie's call center is so I can talk to some of his coworkers. I have to help him, Doug."

"What the hell? Help him?" He's yelling at me now and I have to hold the phone away from my head. "You're going to make things worse for him."

"What are you talking about? No, I'm not!"

"Really? How's it going to look when his *sister* comes to his work and starts asking everyone about these missing people?"

"It's not like th—"

"Think about it, Emmie. Do you really think he's not going to find out what you're up to? And how's he going to feel when he does?"

"Stop! I get it, okay?" I take one deep breath and then another. I remember the promise I made to myself—I can't lose Doug. None of this is worth that—worth the cost of our life together. "I'm sorry," I breathe through the phone. "I don't want to argue about this. I should've told you what I was planning."

I look through the window of the car, watching my parents' neighborhood wake up. Some kids are walking down the sidewalk, heading to school. Couples kiss before getting into their separate cars, heading to work. That's what I want for us. That's all I've ever wanted. If we keep arguing, it's never going to happen.

"Go home," Doug says. "Tell Eddie something came up."

I do as he says. I make my excuses to my brother, who's

probably relieved he doesn't have to explain things to me and head home. The whole time I think nothing but *I hope Doug is right.*

ED

THEN

Sorry, something just came up. Raincheck? Em texts me.

I'm puzzled by my sister, but only for a minute. It's not the strangest thing she's ever done—making plans and then immediately canceling. She probably just had second thoughts about grilling me like our parents. I'm thankful for that.

I check the time and realize there's not enough of it to meet her now, anyway. **Okay**, I send back to her with a thumb up emoji.

At work, I enter the building slouched down, trying to make myself as inconspicuous as possible. I pull my hood from my sweatshirt low over my face, covering as much as it can reach. If they're going to stare, I don't want to see.

No one greets me as I walk to my desk. *Do they ever?* The soft murmur of answering calls fills the room. I strain to hear someone saying something about me but it's hard to tell. *Ignore them.*

I'm in the middle of a call when there's a tap on my shoulder. I startle, thinking it's Adam. *But it can't be*—I turn to see Mark Weber, Adam's supervisor—upper management.

He doesn't smile, just looks at me for a second before mouthing the word "Standby."

I gulp and nod my understanding. *Why would Mark Weber want to see me?* It's hard to focus on the caller but somehow, I manage to get through the rest of our conversation. When the call ends, I take off my headset and look up at Mark, who's still standing behind me, waiting.

"Hi," I say dumbly.

"Come with me, please."

I log out of the computer and follow him into the conference room—the same one I sat in with Adam and the others. Mark directs me to a chair, and I sit, trying not to show how nervous I am. Just like before, there are documents on the table, and I know it can't be good.

"You had a no-call, no-show yesterday," Mark says.

My mouth drops. I'm so shocked that I fumble for words to begin with. "I—yes—I was here."

He frowns at me and checks his papers. "What's your name?"

My face goes red. I've worked here for *eight years.* I've been here twice as long as *Mark.* I've sat in countless meetings with him, *met* him countless times. He's not my immediate boss, but there's no reason he shouldn't know who I am.

I can't keep the irritation from my voice. "Ed Davis."

"Okay. Well, it says here that you weren't here. What time did you clock in?"

I think about it and realize that I *didn't* clock in. I walked into Adam's office and then ran before I had the chance to tell anyone. "I think I know what happened," I say.

He raises his eyebrows and tilts his head, waiting for me to continue.

"I went into Adam's office, and there were police officers in there. When I found out he was missing, I was overcome—I had to leave because I was sick."

Mark purses his lips. "Did you tell anyone?"

"No—but I mean, people saw me. I spoke with one of the officers. I was here."

"Frankly, it doesn't matter if you were *here*, what matters is that you didn't do the job that you were scheduled to do." He flips through some papers. "It looks like Adam has you on notice already."

"But—"

Mark looks straight at me, unflinching, unfeeling. "I'm going to have to let you go."

My future flashes before my eyes. Jobless, stuck with my parents *forever*. My heart starts to race—I can't breathe. I tug at the neck of my hoodie, trying to give my throat more space. I start to pant, trying not to hyperventilate. Blackness is creeping into the sides of my vision.

A look of concern passes over Mark's stone face. He glances at the door, not wanting to be stuck in a room with me if I'm going to freak out. But it's too late.

I stand up, slamming my fists on the table. "This isn't right!" I blink and shake my head. More black is inching in.

"Hey—are you okay?"

"No! I am not okay! This is bullshit!" I stagger back before catching myself on a chair.

"I'll call someone to help you."

"Don't both—" I collapse before I can finish.

EMMIE

THEN

should be at work, I remind myself as I sit on the couch and stare out the window. Doug sits beside me, holding my hand, stroking the back of it like I'm a cat. I want to yank free, but I force myself to hold still.

I can't look at him. That's why I'm looking out the window. My cat comes to us, and rubs against our legs, purring. It gives me an excuse to pull away without starting a fight. Reaching down to scratch his back, I coo, "Hey there, handsome."

When he walks away back to the bedroom, Doug pulls my hand into his again. "Are we done talking about it?" he asks. "I want to be sure you're okay."

I shrug, unable to lie—I promised I wouldn't. But if I tell him what I'm really thinking, we will argue and it's not worth it. "I don't think I can be okay with not trying," I admit. "But I see what you're saying."

"Try to put yourself in Eddie's shoes. How would you feel if he came around work asking questions without asking or telling you first?"

"I know. You're right. I'll think of something else."

"Do you think you can look at me when we're talking?" he says, giving my arm a small tug.

I twist around to meet his eyes, and from the look of them, can't quite tell if he's angry with me. "I'm sorry," I say, reaching to kiss him.

"You're going to drop this obsession with your brother," Doug says.

Anger rises in my chest, but I stay silent. *I don't have an obsession with him,* I think instead, keeping the words inside.

"Yes, you do," he says as if he's heard me. He scowls. "Every time he needs something, you just *have* to go running. Let him be an adult. Let him solve his own problems like you had to."

I turn to look back out the window, but he grabs my face and turns it back to him. "I said look at me when I'm talking to you," Doug says.

My eyes go wide with surprise. "I-I'm sorry."

"So, are we done? You're going to listen to what I'm saying?"

I nod.

"Say something."

"I'll listen. You're right. I don't like it—but I'll listen. I promise."

"You don't like it?" Doug's scowl deepens. "I'm not telling you to cut ties with him. I'm telling you to let him be his own man instead of trying to be his mother."

My heart starts to beat faster with every word he speaks. It gets to the point where I have to hold back tears because he's starting to sound exactly like our dad. I don't even *like him* right now, and everything he says drills that feeling deeper into my heart. I don't want to get to this point—I don't want this feeling to dive any deeper down.

"Can we talk about something else?" I beg. "I just—I don't want to talk about Eddie anymore."

Doug eyes me. "I need to make sure we're on the same page here."

"We are. I *promise* we are."

"Emmie—don't. Don't put me off like that just because you're done. Don't lie to me."

The fingernails on my free hand dig into the side of my thigh. *Don't argue, don't argue, don't argue!* I struggle with what to say to make him understand.

My phone rings. I look at it, then back to Doug. His face says he already knows I'm going to answer, and he's not happy about it. "Let me just see who it is," I say, reaching for it.

It's a number I don't recognize. I show Doug the screen. He nods. "Okay. Answer it."

I slide my finger across the screen. "Hello?" I listen to the woman on the other end of the line. I gasp at what she says. "I'm on my way," I say before hanging up.

"Who was it?" Doug asks.

"That was Eddie's work. He's at the hospital. They called me because I'm his emergency contact." I grip Doug's arm tightly. "Please, Doug. I have to go."

He thinks about it, then finally nods. "Of course you do, Emmie. Go."

ED

When I open my eyes, all I see is white. I touch a hand to my forehead, putting counter-pressure against the ache. There's a bandage across my face. *What the hell happened?*

I turn my head to see a man I don't know in the chair beside my bed. Seeing him sends a jolt through me. I try to sit up but I'm too weak.

The man was reading a novel. Now that I've made movement, he looks up at me. "You're awake," he says.

"Who are you?"

He frowns. "I'm Detective Martinez—we met the other day at your home."

I squint at him. I know his name, but I can't place his face. I don't recognize him at all. When I think back to our meeting before, there's a blank space where his face should be.

"I'm sorry," I say, my face heating. "Why am I here?"

"You passed out at work. Hit your head. Your boss called the police when you started threatening him, so I thought I'd come check in and see how you're doing, have a little chat."

"Threatening him?" My brow creases.

"I'll grab a doctor." He goes to get up, but I stop him.

"Please, I've never threatened anyone in my life—that doesn't sound like me at all." I try to remember what happened. "It's a little hazy. I remember talking with Mark but not threatening him. Are you sure you have the right person?"

"Is your boss Mark?"

"No. Well—I guess so—at the moment, yeah."

"You don't know who your boss is?"

"Of course I do," I say, trying to keep anger from rising in my voice. "My boss is Adam. He's missing. Mark is *his* boss."

Detective Martinez nods, satisfied with my answer. "So… you don't remember your conversation?"

I look at the ceiling, thinking. "We were in the conference room. He—he fired me." It hits me how this must look. *Disgruntled employee—ex-employee—fired. He threatens the boss, falls—or fakes a fall. What's next? Suing his company for a million dollars in damages?*

Our eyes meet. He looks interested in whatever he sees, and it unsettles me. I don't want to be anywhere on his radar. I wait for him to say something.

"Were you upset about that?" the detective asks.

"Yes," I admit. "It was very upsetting."

"But you didn't threaten him?"

"No."

"Maybe you just don't remember?" he asks, arching an eyebrow.

"Does everyone who gets fired threaten their ex-employer?"

The detective's lips thin. I should shut up now. I can tell I'm getting on his bad side.

"Let's talk about your regular boss, Adam."

I'm starting to shake. I hope Martinez doesn't see

because that's only going to make me look guiltier than I already do. "What about him?"

"Do you know anything about where he might be?"

"Why would I know that? We weren't close."

"Are you familiar with the other missing people from your work? Jeremy Oak, Eric Hall, or Brooke Gallagher?"

Here it is. I knew this was going to happen. "Of course I'm familiar with them. I worked with them."

"What was your relationship like?"

"Why are you asking me all this? Do you think I had something to do with their disappearances?"

He shrugs. "Your behavior toward Mark suggests you might be agitated about something. I just want to cover all the bases here."

"Yes, I'm *agitated*." I huff, trying to keep my temper under control. "I'm being questioned by *you* for no reason other than that you don't like my behavior. I was fired for not showing up—but I was *there*. Would you be *agitated* if those things happened to you?"

The detective shifts in his seat. "Okay, Ed. I think this is a bad time. I'll leave you to recover."

Thank you. I release a sigh of relief.

"One more thing," he says before leaving. "I'm not questioning you for nothing, Ed."

I scowl at him.

"We believe you were the last person to see any of the missing individuals before they were reported missing."

He walks out the door.

EMMIE

I grab my things and rush to the car, expecting Doug to be right behind me. When I realize he's not, I turn around to find him still standing in the doorway, watching me. "Aren't you coming?" I call.

"Go on without me," he says. "I'll wait for you here."

I stare at him for a minute, wondering why he refuses to meet Eddie—why he refuses to meet anyone in my family. There's no time to deal with it right now. I turn from him and get in the car.

A nurse leads me to Eddie's room, past a man who just left. He seems somewhat familiar but with his head lowered, I don't get a good look. "The doctor should be in shortly," the nurse says before leaving.

Eddie is lying on a hospital bed, turned on his side, facing away. I hesitate, taking a tentative step toward him. "Eddie?" I ask softly.

He lets out a deep sigh. "Of course they would call you," he says without turning to face me.

"What happened? Your work—"

"They fired me."

"What? Why?" I step forward to stand at the foot of his bed.

"A misunderstanding. It doesn't matter now."

He sounds so lost it breaks my heart. "We'll get this sorted out. We'll talk to someone. It'll—"

"Don't." Eddie rolls over now and at his look of anger, I take a step back. "I have bigger problems than losing my job, Em."

I cringe when I see the bandage across his forehead. It looks like he really hurt himself. "Are you okay? How bad did you hurt yourself?"

"I'm not talking about my fucking face!" he yells. "They think I'm a murderer!"

I bite my lip to hold myself back from peppering him with fifty questions all at once. We stare at each other, him out of breath, me holding mine. I think about what he's said and try to figure it out without asking all that I want to ask.

People from his work are missing. Now, he's getting fired. They think he's a murderer.

"What makes them think it was you?"

"*Apparently,* I was the last person known to be in contact with each of them. *I'm* the link between them."

I go to the side of his bed and crouch so I'm at his level. "Listen to me," I say. "They haven't said anything about finding anyone's body, have they?"

He shakes his head. "No. Not to me."

"Okay. Then they don't have anything to go off of. These people might not even be dead. If they had something solid, they would've arrested you already."

Eddie gives a small nod. "I guess you're right."

"*Were* you the last person to see them?"

"How the hell am I supposed to know? I mean—no, I'm not. Whoever killed them or took them would be, wouldn't they?"

"That's right."

"I just—" He looks away from me and covers his face with his hands.

"What?"

"I'm having—I'm having a hard time remembering some things."

I frown. "Like what?"

"Like, I woke up here in the hospital, but they're acting like I had a full-blown conversation in the ambulance." He throws his hands up. "How is that possible?"

"Has the doctor been in yet? We could ask—"

"I'm *afraid* to ask, Em."

Our eyes meet again. It's so hard to not cry at the look on my brother's face. The anger has been replaced by a soul-deep fear. He's afraid of himself—of what he might find out if he asks.

"I'm here for you. No matter what."

"What am I going to do?" he chokes out.

"There's only one thing to do. You have to live your life. Don't let this get in the way. This is nothing, Eddie. In a few weeks, they'll move on to harassing their next suspect."

"The only reason the detective showed up was because someone from work called him."

So that's who that was leaving Eddie's room. The thought infuriates me. He's injured—maybe badly—and they come to hound him—can't even wait until he's home. "I'm going to speak with someone and complain about their policies here. He should've never been allowed in to see you."

I turn to walk back out in search of someone but before I make it two steps, a doctor steps through the door.

ED

"How are you feeling?" the doctor asks, eyeing me carefully.

"My head hurts a little," I say, not wanting to mention my memory loss.

"That's understandable. We had to give you ten stitches —you had a nasty fall there. The pain should ease up in a couple of days, though. I'll prescribe you some painkillers so you can sleep at night."

Ten stitches? Across my forehead? My stomach churns.

"Do you have any questions for me?" she asks.

My eyes flick to Em. She gives me an encouraging look, urging me to say something else about how I'm feeling. My hands grasp each other in a death-grip on my lap. It's on the tip of my tongue to say something, *anything* that might help me understand but I'm too worried about what it means.

The doctor checks her watch. She raises an eyebrow at me, rushing to move on to the next patient in line. "I—um —" I look at Em one more time for encouragement. "I don't really remember being in the ambulance," I finally admit. I decide to stick with a half-truth, not divulging the rest of my memory problems.

The doctor nods. "Okay, that can be normal. Do you remember what happened before you were hurt?"

"Yes. I was—" My face turns beet red. "I was getting fired."

She nods again. "And after that, what's the next thing you remember?"

"Waking up here, in this room."

She looks at me a little too closely for my comfort, making me squirm. Her eyes scan mine as she thinks about the situation. "You could have had enough stress to induce short-term memory loss, especially accompanied by a head injury. We can run some tests to see if there was more damage, but judging by the extent of your injuries, you may want to speak with a mental health expert. Do you have a therapist or psychiatrist already?"

Therapist. Psychiatrist. She says the words so casually—throwing them out there in the wind. Why would she think I have one already? Is it that obvious there's something else wrong with me?

I start to panic. *I don't want to be crazy!* Em's voice breaks through. "Doctor, I didn't know stress could cause memory loss."

The doctor turns to her. "Yes, with a significant amount and the other factors involved, it's a definite possibility."

I start to relax. *What if all the memory problems I've been having are just because of the stress?* Stress. That's it. I nod at the doctor. "I don't want any tests. I think you're right. I was really, really stressed."

"Are you sure?" she asks.

"Yep. Sure, I'm sure."

"You might remember what happened in a few more hours or a few days. More than likely, this is temporary."

I doubt it. "Thank you, doctor."

Em and I are sitting in her car an hour later. She wants to bring me home, but I can't do that to her. I swore to myself that I wouldn't burden her anymore and look at me—doing exactly what I swore I wouldn't do.

"I'll make us something special to eat," she says. "Anything you want. You're probably starved."

"Thanks, but just drop me off at my hotel."

"Your *hotel*?"

"Yeah. I got a room after—you know," I say, thinking about the detective showing up at the house.

Em nods. "Why didn't you come over? You know you're welcome to stay as long as you need."

My lips thin. I don't answer.

"I'm sorry," she whispers.

Minutes later, Em pulls in front of my hotel, ready to drop me off. "You know what—" I say before opening the door. "I'm going to check out of this stupid place. Just wait for me, okay? My car isn't here—it's still at work—or they probably had it towed, who knows."

She pauses. "Okay—I mean—are you sure?"

No. "Yeah. I can't stay here forever. I'm sure they're calmed down by now anyway and besides, I can just lock myself in my room if I have to," I say, *dreading* walking through the front door. "And I'll worry about the stupid car later."

I can tell Em wants to say something but instead she just nods. It doesn't take me long to check out—I didn't have anything with me to begin with. We ride in silence that feels strained—both wanting to say the right thing, neither knowing what that right thing is.

"I'm going to see a therapist," I say. I don't know why I

say it other than that I don't want her to think the worst of me.

She nods absently, keeping her eyes on the road. We pull up to the curb in front of our parents' house, and Em's eyes widen. I look out the window and choke back a scream. *Detective Martinez is here.*

We wait, letting the quiet stretch between us, watching through the windshield. "What do you want to do?" I ask.

"Just wait a minute."

So, we wait. Neither of us speaks for ten minutes—when it becomes clear that the detective isn't there to speak with Eddie. He's there to speak to our parents—*about* Eddie.

We can see them through the living room window, all sitting comfortably, chatting like they were old friends. "What do you think they're saying?" I ask.

Eddie's fists clench on his lap. "Let's go."

"We could—"

"*Please*, Em."

He sounds like he's going to either scream or cry, so I decide to keep my mouth shut. I know Eddie—he'll need to process this in his own way. This detective isn't letting up for whatever reason but there's nothing we can do about it.

I don't ask where he wants to go. I'm sure he regrets checking out of his hotel room—I could take him back to get another. That's nonsense though. Until he tells me otherwise, I'm taking him home with me.

We park and make our way to the front door. Eddie doesn't complain that I've brought him here. I put my key in the door, but it's already unlocked.

I brighten—Doug is still here. He waited for me like he said he would. I turn to Eddie, grinning despite everything.

"What are you so happy about?" he asks.

"Doug is here. You want to meet him?"

He shrugs. "Why not. He's here—I'm here. It's about time, isn't it?"

I hug him tight and kiss him on the cheek. We walk through the door together. "Doug?" I call.

"Just a minute," he yells from the bedroom.

I smile at Eddie. "Mind if I get some water?" he asks, moving to the fridge.

"You know you don't have to ask, silly. There's some beer in there too if you want."

"Thanks."

I hear the rattle of the glass bottles and Doug's footsteps coming from down the hall. "Hey beautiful, how'd everything go?" he says, coming to me, giving me a deep kiss.

When he pulls away, I'm flushed. "Eddie is here. Let me introduce you," I whisper to him. I look toward Eddie, still in the kitchen, but he's already staring at us.

"Eddie, this is Doug. Doug—this is my brother, Eddie." I laugh. "But you know he hates that name, so you better stick with calling him Ed."

"Ed." Doug nods with a warm smile.

We wait for Eddie to say something but he's just standing there, grinding his jaw, looking like he wants to punch a wall. He slams his beer on the counter, and I cringe at the sound of the glass against the countertop.

He steps out of the kitchen, moving toward us. "Is this some kind of fucking joke, Em?"

Doug moves in front of me. I can tell he doesn't want to get in the middle of a brother-sister fight, but he still wants Eddie to respect me. "It's okay," I say, touching his arm.

"I'm just going to wait in the bedroom," he says, giving Eddie a warning look. "Let me know if you need me."

I kiss him before he goes, and when I do, I hear the sound of Eddie popping his knuckles. Doug leaves. I look at Eddie running his hands through his hair. He's whispering something to himself, looking up at the ceiling.

"What the hell, Eddie? That was so rude. What's your problem?"

He stares at me, and I think he's going to scream. He doesn't though. Instead, he hugs me and says, "I have to go."

"What? Eddie—"

"I'll explain later. I just—I have to go."

I move to get the keys, but he stops me. "I'll walk."

I start to cry. "Eddie, tell me what's going on. You're acting like you know Doug already."

He only shakes his head. "I have to go, Em."

***

I watch Eddie through the window, walking away into the horizon. The moment he set eyes on Doug, something changed. *He knows him. He has to.* What else would explain his reaction?

And Doug didn't say, "It's nice to meet you." He said, "Ed," like you would greet an acquaintance. Why would neither of them tell me that they've met before?

Anger fills me to the brim. I want to yell at Doug. I want to go track Eddie down and demand answers. I clench my fists, my fingernails digging into my palms. *Remember, no fighting.*

I groan, knowing I can't go into the bedroom and start yelling at Doug. I don't want to start a fight over something that doesn't really matter. They know each other—so what? They didn't tell me—fine.

I take a deep breath and then head into the bedroom. Doug is on the bed, watching TV. "Did he leave?" he asks.

"I'm—sorry for his behavior. I don't know what got into him."

Doug shrugs. "It's okay."

"Do you—" I twist my lips, unsure how to ask. Then I decide not to beat around the bush. "Do you guys know each other already?"

He looks at me, confused. "Why on earth would you think that? No. We don't know each other." He turns back to the TV.

I bite my lip. *He's never going to admit it. Don't bother.* "He was really upset for some reason—"

"I could tell."

"I think I should find him and talk to him."

Doug mutes the TV, then looks at me again. He sighs. "We just talked about this."

"This is different. He's hurt, he's upset—he needs someone to talk to."

"Let him breathe a little. What he needs is to blow off some steam."

I can hear my heartbeat in my ears. I'm torn, unsure what to do. I look down at my stomach. All this stress can't possibly be good for the baby.

Doug follows my line of vision. His eyes soften. "How are you feeling?"

"I'm fine. I'm just—I want to be there for Eddie."

He turns cold. "I told you already—"

"Please, Doug," I say with tears in my eyes. "I don't want to fight about this. I love you so much—"

His face is starting to turn red with anger. He's gripping the remote so tight, it looks like he might snap it. "Are you an idiot?" he says.

My mouth falls open, stunned into silence.

"You must be. Because you can't get it through your thick fucking skull." Doug stands and when he comes toward me, I back myself into a wall. "If you walk out that door right now, there are going to be consequences. Are you willing to live with them?"

I can't hold the tears back anymore. He's so cold, so hard. It's like he's a total stranger. I don't know who this man is but I'm powerless to fight him. I shake my head. "I won't go," I whisper.

"Good girl," he says. Then he moves to sit back down on the bed and finish his show.

I leave the room, unable to bear looking at him. I lay on the couch, wallowing in self-pity, worried about Eddie. It doesn't take long before I hear Doug snoring. He's so off his normal schedule that he's fallen asleep sitting up. It's not the first time it's happened.

Now's my chance. As quietly as I can, I find the car keys and sneak out of my own house. I'm going to find my brother.

ED

THEN

can't believe this, I can't believe this, I can't believe this! I repeat the words over and over in my mind as I walk home. Either Em is playing some kind of sick joke on me or she has no clue. I don't think she's that good of an actress, so I'm leaning toward her having no idea what's going on.

The thought makes me even angrier because I should've been there for her. I should've cared enough to meet her man before now. *And a baby!* I spit on the ground.

I've been too wrapped up in my own problems. She's been so worried about me when I should've been there for her. I have to protect her. I have to get home and get my thoughts together—then I have to get my car somehow.

It's not too late, I remind myself. I can still do something about *Doug.*

"Where on earth have you been?" my mom yells as soon as she sets eyes on me. Detective Martinez is gone, taking with him any hopes I had of my mom being calm and rational today.

"I stayed at a hotel," I say, moving to my room. It's taken me hours to walk home. I'm tired, hot, and all I want is to clean up and be left alone. I'm not in the mood for my mom's interrogation.

"Who'd you stay with?" *he* asks.

I keep walking, not willing to acknowledge the question.

"Larry, do something!" my mom screams when I keep walking.

"Get the fuck over here," *he* growls at me. I freeze, the same old fear that's always been there, never willing to go away even after all these years, creeps up my spine.

I turn back toward them, my ears feeling like they're on fire. "I prefer not to talk about this right now. *Please.*"

He slams his fist into the wall he's standing next to. My mom and I both jump. "The next one goes into your face," he snarls.

I take a step toward my mom. "What do you want to know, Mom?"

"Kate is missing."

My ears start ringing.

"I want to know what's going on. The police seem to think you're guilty of something, and I want you to tell me all about it. You have no idea how embarrassing it was for me to have a detective show up asking questions about you, Edward!" She waves her hand in front of her face as if to cool herself down. "Now Kate—"

Neither of them has mentioned the large bandage across my forehead. Neither has asked if I'm okay. They don't care. All they care about is how this is going to affect *them*.

I clench my jaw. "They think I have something to do with some missing people."

"I *know!* How can that be? Are you guilty?"

I try not to roll my eyes in annoyance. If she already knows everything, why is she making me say anything at all? Every word out of her mouth is a high-pitched scream, drilling deeper and deeper into my brain. I wish she would just *stop*.

"No. I'm not guilty."

"I don't believe you," *he* says. "Do you, Shawna?"

Mom frowns, staring straight at me. "No. I don't either, Larry."

I'm not sure I've ever felt so alone in my entire life. "If you don't believe me—fine. There's nothing I can do about that. But I'm innocent."

"Stop lying to us!" my mom cries.

The front door opens, and my eyes gravitate to Em coming in. *Great.* Neither of my parents notice her. She's quiet, staying out of our argument.

"What did you do to them? You need to confess to the police. Stop wasting everyone's time," *he* says.

"Edward, tell your father what you did with those people. What you did to *Kate*," she chokes. "Stop this nonsense. I'm going to call Detective Martinez so we can finally get everything out in the open."

I'm starting to feel lightheaded and dizzy. I stumble and catch myself before I fall.

"What the hell is wrong with you now?" *he* screams at me. "Are you *high*? Did you come into my house on drugs?" He takes a step toward me, looking like he wants to break my nose.

"I'm not—"

A drop of blood falls from my nose. *Great, a bloody nose —just what I need right now.*

I park, ready to get out of the car, but before I can reach for the door handle, a hard knock comes at the passenger window. I look and have to stifle a scream. Doug is here. *How the hell is he here?*

He looks angry but doesn't sound it when he speaks. "Come on," he says.

I get out and go to him. "What are you doing here?"

"I knew you couldn't resist." He sighs. "I may as well be with you. I can meet your parents now so everyone can hate me, not just your brother."

"Don't say that." I pull him to me and hug him. "Thank you for being here."

"I don't like it. I don't like that you tried to go behind my back, but with everything going on—I'm not going to let you be here alone."

We approach the door, then hear the yelling. Doug and I share a look. I knock hard, trying to distract them from each other. We wait. No one answers—they continue screaming at Eddie.

I look up at Doug, question in my eyes. I feel a headache

coming on. Doug twists the door handle—it's not locked. We step inside.

Their voices make me cringe. I'm so embarrassed that Doug has to see this—it's so intimate, so private. Will he even want to be a part of this family now? I put a protective hand to my baby, wanting to shield it, even though I know it's safe inside me.

I lead Doug to the kitchen so he can sit down away from the madness. Then Eddie starts to bleed. Daddy is over him. I feel faint. I close my eyes for a moment, trying to clear my foggy mind. *What the hell is happening?*

When I open my eyes, everything is silent. *Finally, they've stopped.* I release a sigh filled with tension. But then I realize something is terribly wrong.

Eddie is *covered* in blood. He's holding a knife—staring at me in horror. At his feet are our parents. Dead. "Oh my god, Eddie," I whisper.

I swivel to look at Doug in the kitchen but he's not there. "Where's Doug?" I ask, unable to think of anything else.

Eddie shakes his head. "Not here."

I frown. My hands shake but I reach for the knife he's still holding. "What happened, Eddie? Are you hurt?"

He backs up and wards me off with his free hand. "Don't."

"Okay. Okay." I back away, not wanting him to unleash his fury on me.

"Is Doug okay?" I ask, dreading the possibility that Eddie killed him too.

"Don't worry about *Doug*," Eddie hisses. "Look at our parents!"

I start to cry. He's right. I stare at them, feeling light-headed again at the sight of all the blood. It's all over every-thing—the walls, the couches, the floors. Eddie's hands are so soaked through, I think the blood might never be washed clean.

The air is filled with the smell. My eyes dart to each of our parents' bodies and around the room—I can't stop looking at *everything*. Tears fill my eyes. Our world has been shattered in an instant.

I jump when Eddie grabs my shoulders, no longer holding the knife. Our eyes meet. I've never been afraid of my brother—I've always known he wouldn't hurt me. But now, I don't know what to think. I never thought he would break like this.

"What did you do to Doug?" I whisper. He was right here next to me—was just *here*. How can he be gone?

His lips thin. "I didn't do anything to him."

"Then where is he?"

"He—" Eddie looks away, looks everywhere but at me. "He—he went home."

"*Why?*" We hear sirens in the distance. How are they coming so soon? I look at Eddie, panicked, but he seems so calm. "Eddie, we have to do something."

He shakes his head. "No."

I cry harder. "You have to tell them it was an accident. Make sure they understand it wasn't your fault!"

He says nothing. He's staring at me now, contemplating.

"I can't lose you, Eddie! I love you!"

Tears fall to his cheeks. I throw myself into him, grasping on to him until the police come inside. "She didn't do anything," Eddie says, his hands raised in the air. Then they take him away from me.

I've spent so much time explaining to Dr. Reymore about Doug. He's watched me with understanding eyes, nodding along with my story, and I don't believe he's faking his concern.

Now that he knows his history and why I'm so worried about my sister's wellbeing, I have true hope that Dr. Reymore will do something to help. He can call the police, tell whoever he needs to tell, do *something* to help her.

"So—you'll do something about him?" I ask, needing to get confirmation that Em is going to be safe now.

Dr. Reymore purses his lips. "I appreciate you giving me his history. It's very insightful. But—before I can do anything… I want you to tell me about that day from your own eyes. Not what the police believe, not what your sister believes, what *you* believe happened. Can you do that, Ed?"

I frown a little, not wanting to paint Em in a bad light. By the look on his face, I can tell he's eager to help as much as he can, though, and I know I have to talk. *To help her*, I have to speak the truth.

"Okay," I finally say. "I'll tell you."

ED

THEN

"Larry, my *floors!*" my mom wails, seeing the blood drop from my nose onto her freshly cleaned carpet.

He comes toward me, reaching for my face. "Don't lean backward," he says, pulling my head forward. He bunches up his shirt sleeve and holds it up to me. I flinch back, thinking he means to hit me—but he doesn't.

The next second, he's screaming in agony. My eyes widen as I try to figure out what's happening. Em is behind him, a look of pure rage on her face. "Leave him alone!" she screams in a guttural cry. She raises a serrated knife and plunges it into him. The sound of it cutting against his flesh makes me lightheaded.

"Em, don't—" I say. But it's too late.

I'm hypnotized by her. She stabs him over and over before moving to our mom. Mom tries to fight back but doesn't stand a chance against Em's fury.

Em is swinging the knife around, slicing both of our parents into pieces like she's preparing a meal. My stomach heaves. I look away to take a steadying breath.

No amount of effort on my part will stop her. I recognize the look in her eyes and if I get in the way—it'll be me on the floor bleeding too, whether she intends it or not. I have no choice but to stay out of it and watch my sister cut away the last semblance of the life we know.

I've known she was sick for a long time now. I didn't know what it was at first—tried to ignore it. I hoped she was better by now. She seemed so—so—okay.

Deep down, I know she would never hurt me... or at least, would never *intentionally* hurt me. When we were kids—they thought it was me who cut myself. I let them think it. She still believes it. She's my sister—we're supposed to protect our siblings, aren't we?

When it's over, she lets me take the knife from her bloody grip. She stands frozen, almost comatose, staring at their bodies. My teeth grind together as I think of what to do. I don't know if she's had a full mental break or is just in shock.

I call 9-1-1. There's no other choice. When I hang up, she's still out of it, so I stand beside her, waiting for as long as she needs.

Her eyes widen, and suddenly I think it dawns on Em what's happened. She looks at me and—asks about *Doug.* Inside my head, I'm screaming. *Doug, Doug, Doug! Fucking Doug!*

"He went home," I manage to say, wanting to say so much more—*needing* to say so much more.

But then the sirens come. And Em says, "You have to tell them it was an accident. Make sure they understand it wasn't your fault!" She looks at my hand, covered in blood, still holding the dripping knife.

I realize what I have to do. I have to let them think it was me again. I have to let *her* think it. Because if she knows the truth—that Doug doesn't even *exist* and that *she* did this, not me—there might not be any of my sister left.

I clench my fists by my side, keeping my eyes on my lap. My throat is tight. My stomach clenches. *I hope I made the right decision.*

"Thank you for telling me," Dr. Reymore says. "I'm sure this must be very difficult for you. Tell me—" He adjusts his glasses. "How does it feel to be locked away, believing you didn't commit this terrible crime?"

Believing. The word hits me like a slap to the face. I look up to meet his gaze. I swallow. It's not *concern* I saw there before. No, I was wrong. It's *curiosity.*

"You don't believe me."

He smiles. "What I believe doesn't matter. What matters is what *you* believe."

I break out in a cold sweat. The realization dawns on me. Dr. Reymore might not help me *or* Em. He might not believe a word I've said.

I start to take deep breaths—in… hold—out… repeat. *I'm okay*—the thought is cut off short.

They let her visit me the next day. Her eyes are red rimmed with purple bags beneath. It's obvious she hasn't been sleeping. *I haven't either.*

I've been thinking about what she said before—*you shouldn't live the rest of your life not getting the help you need.* I can't bear to see her in pain, but I don't think that's going to change no matter what I do. "Em—there's something I need to tell you."

"What is it? What's wrong?"

"Things—things didn't happen the way the police think they happened."

She frowns. "I was there—I saw."

I give a slow nod. "Yes. You saw. You did more than that too. Do you remember?"

Her forehead scrunches as she thinks. Her eyes dart between mine. "I—"

"You killed them," I whisper.

"I—" She shakes her head, filled with confusion.

"No. It was you, Eddie. I heard the yelling—the—the blood."

"No, *dammit!* Think about it, Em. Remember what happened. *You* had the knife. You cut *him* first, then her. I took the knife from you *afterward.*"

Em's eyes glaze over as she tries to remember that day. The day our parents were murdered.

I see myself standing at the front door, listening to the screaming inside. My face is so hot, I feel like I could melt. Doug is by my side, listening to everything my parents are yelling at Eddie. When I look over at him with a grimace, his face is flushed too.

"Are you just going to stand here and do nothing?" he asks.

"I—no." I try the door handle. It's unlocked. The door swings open. I take Doug's hand in mine and pull him through the entryway.

"What did you do to them? You need to confess to the police. Stop wasting everyone's time." Spittle flying from Daddy's mouth, and it looks like he's ready to hit Eddie. He grabs him by the front of his shirt and pulls him close in a death grip.

"Edward, tell your father what you did with those people. What you did to *Kate*. Stop this nonsense. I'm going to call Detective Martinez." Mom's voice is shrill, panicked. She's not as loud as Daddy but her tone makes her voice carry easier, drilling into my eardrums.

Neither of them believes Eddie. They both think he's

guilty. When I look at Eddie's eyes, full of defensive anger and confusion—so alone, I feel so sad. I hate that he's going through this. His life was hard enough before. I've only been trying to help him, but I think I've done a really bad job at it.

Eddie tries to pull himself out of Daddy's firm grip. When Mom's piercing voice rings out right next to his ear, he winces and turns his head to face her. "I didn't do anything to any—"

She slaps him open palmed across his face. A bright red outline of her hand is left behind. "Stop lying to us!" she demands.

"You can't let them keep treating him this way," Doug says next to me.

I grip his hand. "I'm sorry you have to see this."

"We need to put an end to it."

"They won't listen to me. They don't listen to anyone but themselves."

Eddie tries pulling himself free again. He pushes against Daddy's shoulders, twisting and yanking furiously. He's almost slipped out of his shirt when Daddy starts swinging his fist. He hits Eddie in the stomach, causing him to double over and gasp.

I cringe and bite my lip at the sight. They're all too busy to notice my presence. *Why won't Mom put an end to this violence?* This is *not* the way to get Eddie to talk.

"Hey!" I see myself calling to them. "What's going on?"

Only Eddie turns to look at me. "Em," he chokes. "Don't—"

"Don't worry about her, goddammit," Daddy says. He punches Eddie again, this time in the jaw. Eddie's hands fly up to protect himself. He stumbles from the blow and a few drops of blood drip out of his mouth.

"Larry! What are you doing to my carpet? He's bleeding all over it!"

"You wanted me to get answers out of him, didn't you? Let me do what I need to do!"

"But my *floors*! Edward Michael, you tell us right this damn minute where those bodies are!" She reaches up and grabs a fist full of his hair. Eddie cries out but Mom doesn't let go.

"They're going to kill him," Doug whispers.

My eyes are watering. I'm like a deer that's frozen in the headlights. I see what's happening but I'm too shocked, too terrified to do anything about it. Never in my life have I seen my parents behave this way, especially not to Eddie.

"Emmie, do something," Doug says when I don't respond. I finally break myself out of my trance and move to the kitchen. I see myself reaching for a knife from the knife block on the counter, not paying attention to which one I grab.

I hold it up, seeing the long serrated blade. "Will you leave him alone!" I cry. I hold the knife up to my opposite arm. "I'll cut myself if you don't stop!"

They still don't pay any attention to me. They're too consumed with getting answers out of Eddie. "I will *not* have a murderer as a son!" Mom yells. She slaps Eddie again, even harder this time. He has blood coming out of both nostrils, leaking to the carpet and setting her off on a tangent about her precious floors again.

The more they hit him, the angrier they become, feeding their own fury and crazy ideas. Eddie is still trying to get away, but he's helpless with the two of them ganging up on him with their fury.

He's on the floor now and he pushes Mom away when she kneels beside him in order to slap him again. Daddy lashes out. "Don't you *dare* touch her!" He kicks Eddie several times in the abdomen, groin, and legs.

"They're going to kill him!" Doug cries louder now. I

meet his worried gaze. Wiping the tears from my eyes, I beg him. "Help Eddie, Doug, please!"

"You have to do something," he says. "He's your brother. Your *twin*, Emmie. He's the most important person in your life. *Help him.*"

"I can't! They won't listen!" I swipe at my face again, desperate to clear my blurry vision.

"Do something! You have to do something! They're killing him!" Doug cries again. He doesn't stop. A relentless, never-ending cry that echoes on and on in my mind. *They're going to kill Eddie.*

I take one last look at him lying helpless on the floor while my parents beat the life out of him. Then I grip the knife tighter and move.

"Stop it!" I wail in a blood-curdling scream, an arm's reach away from Daddy. I see myself swinging the knife around and *feel* the serrated blade slice into his flesh. He yells out in pain, but I cut again, sawing into his back before he has a chance to turn around.

"Emersyn!" my mom screams. She moves to stand up, but I watch myself swing the knife across her chest before she gets the chance. A jagged chasm opens up above her breasts, spilling a fountain of blood onto the floor next to Eddie.

"Watch out!" Doug cries.

I swing back around without looking, cutting Daddy across his arms. I can see his meat and almost gag at the sight, but I'm still too furious. They deserve this for what they've done to Eddie. I look at Daddy in the eyes, then stab him straight through his stomach. I'm lost to myself— no longer thinking, only feeling. Feeling every single ounce of pain they put him through.

His mouth sags open with shock. I watch as I pull the blade out and saw into him again and again, not stopping until there's no more visible canvas to cut.

"Em." Eddie's weak voice makes me turn just in time.

Mom is there with a lamp raised to bring down on me. She throws it and misses. It was her last chance. "Think about all the times she could have stopped him," Doug says.

"You're right."

Mom looks at me in confusion. "About what?" she asks.

Too late for explanations. I cut her again and again until there's nothing left to cut.

Tears fall freely from Em's eyes. "Doug—he—he told me to do it?"

I nod. "You wondered where he went after."

"All those people," she says. "The ones from your work."

I nod again.

"What happened to them?"

I shrug. "You were just trying to help me. You wanted me to be—free of them. I told you what each of them did to me, remember? You couldn't stand the way I was being treated. Doug told you to do something about them too."

"Even the woman—"

"Brooke."

"Yeah. Her. I thought you—liked her a lot."

"I did. I do. But you didn't see it that way. You—believed she was playing a game with me."

More tears fall from Em's eyes. "Eddie—"

"Shh. You don't have to say anything, Em. I just wanted to get everything out in the open. I want you to get the help you need—the help you *deserve*."

She shakes her head. "No, Eddie. I'm *pregnant*."

"Are you?" I tilt my head to the side, letting her think about it. "Your stomach hasn't grown at all… how far along are you?"

Em bites her lip. "The test was positive. I *know* there's a baby, Eddie."

I hate to see her in such agony, but if I don't spell this out for her, she's never going to get better. I should've told her that day. I was such an idiot to think that hiding it from her would be protecting her. "People have false readings all the time—false pregnancies even. Your body might've believed it was pregnant, but in reality—you weren't. I'm sorry, Em."

She shakes her head at me again. "Why are you doing this? *Why*, Eddie?"

My throat feels so dry my words come out in a rasp. I feel like I'm torturing her, and I'm not sure I'll be able to live with myself after this. More than her pain though, I know her words will always haunt me if I don't tell her the truth.

"It's like you said before. I just want you to get the care you need, Em."

"That's why you didn't like him before. Isn't it? The day I introduced you to Doug?"

My lips flatten. "He's not *real*, Em."

"Have you—decided what you're going to do?"

"I told my doctor everything. He's going to help us."

She nods. A look passes over her face that I can't read. "I love you, Eddie."

"I love you too, Em," I choke out, trying to keep my emotions in check.

"I want to speak to your doctor. Is that okay?"

Relief floods my body in a wave. I smile, proud of her for making a hard decision. I was willing to go to jail for the rest of my life to protect her. But I'm so glad now that I saw the error of my logic. It's not about going to jail or being locked up. It's about her getting the help she needs. She can't live the rest of her life seeing hallucinations—seeing people who aren't really there. She needs to come to terms with what she did.

She was the one who talked me into doing this, and I'm so grateful. I don't know what the rest of my life is going to look like now—something far different than what I've come to accept—but I'm determined to spend the rest of it making sure she's getting better.

"Of course it's okay for you to talk to him," I say, releasing a deep breath.

EMMIE

NOW
A YEAR LATER

We sit on our bench overlooking the Puget Sound. It's the same one Eddie used to love. I hold my baby in my arms and smile up at Doug next to me with an arm around my shoulders.

We ignore the stares. People *always* stare. It's always made me uncomfortable, but now it doesn't matter.

"I wish Eddie was here," I sigh.

"He's getting the help he needs," Doug says.

"I know. It's just hard."

He hasn't dropped it yet—even now. I never knew how lost he was until that day I visited him. He was going to tell them *I did it*. How could he do that to me? I shake my head at the memory.

Beneath my baby, my hand grips the last letter that Eddie sent. "Do you want me to do it?" Doug asks softly.

"No. Just hold Eddie." I give our child to Doug. We gave him my brother's name—the name *I* love. "I can't believe he tried to tell me this wasn't real," I say.

I could almost laugh if it wasn't so heartbreaking. He had me believing there was something wrong with Doug— that he was malicious somehow. And then he dropped a bombshell on me. *Like I was going to allow him to ruin my life when all I've ever done is devote mine to protecting him.*

The letter is half crumpled. I stretch it flat to read Eddie's words.

> *Em—*
> *Please see the truth.*
> *I can't stay in here. I thought I could, but I was wrong.*
> *Please don't do this to me.*
> *Ask Doug where the bodies are.*
> *I love you.*
> *—Eddie*

Short and sweet. But it's the only time he's referred to himself as that. *Eddie.* I frown at the words. I don't like them. I wish they would stop him from doing this to me.

Sighing, I stand from the bench and take a few steps toward the edge of the lookout. I've done this with every letter he's sent. I crumple the paper back into a ball and throw it over the ledge, watching it soar into the water below.

It floats for a brief second before the water overtakes it and it sinks under. Tears well in my eyes, but I fight them back. I turn back to Doug, still holding little Eddie.

"Let's go," I say. We walk together, still ignoring the stares on the way back to the car.

ED

NOW

They don't believe me. Not my so-called doctor, not Em, not *anyone*. I'm helpless in here. I try to resign myself to the fate that I once accepted. It's not so bad, I tell myself. It's better than prison after all, right?

I see Brooke's face every day. Every morning when I open my eyes, every night when I close them, I picture her and what our life might've been like. Anger and betrayal always surface before I shove them back down where they came from. The only thing those feelings bring is the memory of our last conversation—how she didn't *know* me —how I was *bothering* her—how she *regretted* being with me. I'd rather focus on the positive.

I write to Em once a month, begging her to reconsider what she's doing—what she's done. They tell me they still haven't found the bodies. Dr. Reymore asks me every session if I remember what I did with them—they'll never understand.

I always think about it, just to appease him. During our sessions, I think about the last time I saw each of those people at work, and Kate—and it's like there's a blank spot where the memory should be. It doesn't matter if I remember when I saw them anyway. I didn't do this.

"It was Em," I always remind him. "Not me."

He makes a little note on his paper, and I say, "Why hasn't anyone asked her where she put them? Why won't you talk to her?"

"We have talked to your sister, Ed."

My eyes light up. "What did she say?"

"She told us what really happened, but it's not just her word against yours—you remember the trial, don't you?"

I clench my jaw. "Yes." *Of course I remember the trial.*

Dr. Reymore nods. "Then you know there's evidence to consider."

"Damn the evidence," I say. "I grabbed the knife from her! Haven't you been listening?"

He frowns and makes another note. Then he sighs. "You've been here a year, Ed. I had hoped by now we would've made some progress."

I stay silent—hating this man. I hate to look at him, hate everything that he stands for. He's supposed to be helping me. He's supposed to believe me when I tell him something. What's the point in asking if he's just going to assume I'm wrong? I'm in here, and I'm automatically seen as being insane—having no grip on reality. It doesn't matter whether or not I actually do.

"Let's try a different approach," he says. "I want you to think about your home—living with your parents. What are some words you would use to describe it? Tell me what you see, smell, taste in your mind when you think about it."

With my lips pursed, I close my eyes to think. I picture the house in my mind—being inside, alone.

"Where did you spend the most time?" Dr. Reymore asks.

"My bedroom. I was only home to sleep if I could help it."

"Tell me what it looked like there."

"My walls were bare—plain white. The paint was chipping on the corner by the door because I always bumped into it when I left in a hurry. My closet had some paint missing there too. I'm not sure what that was from. That's where the crawlspace was—maybe the door hit the wall too many times or something."

"Why would the crawlspace be used that often?"

I shrug. "It's an old house," I say as if that answers it. We haven't lived there forever. How the hell am I supposed to know.

"What did your room smell like?" he asks.

"I had these little air fresheners Em gave me all the time. They smelled like the ocean. She knew that was my favorite."

"That was thoughtful of her."

"Yeah—" My face turns red with embarrassment. "She was too nice to say it, but my room smelled without them."

Dr. Reymore turns his head in thought. "What did it smell like without them?"

"Kind of musky, I guess. Probably my body odor—it didn't smell good."

"You didn't seem to have body odor when we first met —even after you'd been in prison for weeks."

"Well, my room stank, okay. It smelled like I left something bad under the bed, and it was rot—" I suck in a breath. My eyes fly open to meet his.

He's staring at me intently, knowing what I'm about to say.

"It smelled like something was rotting," I say numbly.

He nods.

"The bodies are under the house."

THANK YOU!

ACKNOWLEDGMENTS

I want to thank my husband and son for being my biggest supporters. Thank you for always believing in me and cheering me on, for holding me up on my worst days, and standing by my side on my best. I'm so blessed to have both of you. I love you to infinity and beyond.

To my editor and proofreader at My Brother's Editor, thank you for helping me take my vision and make it shine.

To the bookish community—readers, authors, editors, etc., all of you—thank you for all your continued support and encouragement, not just for me, but for all writers and authors. Never in my life have I been a part of a community so helpful and encouraging, and it's the most amazing thing. I could not be where I am today without you.

And to you, dear reader, thank you for showing your support in my writing by reading this book. Whether you are new to my work or are coming back for more, I truly hope you enjoyed the read.

ALSO BY K. LUCAS

The Wrong Stranger

The Neighbors

Rainier

ABOUT K. LUCAS

K. Lucas is an author who lives for the unexpected twist. Originally from California, she now lives in the Pacific Northwest with her husband, son, three dogs, cat, chickens, and ducks. After earning a bachelor's degree in information technology, she became a homeschool mom and then a full-time author. She loves all things thrilling & chilling, and her favorite pastimes include reading, watching scary movies, and exploring nature.

www.klucasauthor.com

CONNECT WITH K. LUCAS

See K. Lucas's website for more info, signed copies, and to sign up for newsletter updates!

Website:
www.klucasauthor.com

Newsletter:
www.klucasauthor.com/newslettersignup

amazon.com/author/klucas

goodreads.com/klucas

bookbub.com/authors/k-lucas

instagram.com/author_klucas

facebook.com/author.klucas

tiktok.com/@klucasauthor

twitter.com/AuthorKLucas

pinterest.com/klucasauthor